This book belongs to:

_____

_____

A TREASURY OF
MAGICAL
STORIES

Over 80 wonderful tales

This edition published by Parragon Books Ltd in 2017

Parragon Books Ltd
Chartist House
15–17 Trim Street
Bath BA1 1HA, UK
www.parragon.com

ISBN 978-1-4748-7086-3

Printed in China

A TREASURY OF
MAGICAL
STORIES

Over 80 wonderful tales

PaRragon

Bath • New York • Cologne • Melbourne • Delhi
Hong Kong • Shenzhen • Singapore

Contents

The Little Mermaid

Far, far out to sea, where the water is crystal clear, lies a secret kingdom. Here a mer-king lived with his six mermaid daughters.

The youngest was a quiet girl, with a gentle heart. She dreamed of faraway adventures in the world above the sea.

"Once a mermaid is fifteen," said her grandmother, "she is allowed to swim up to the surface. Be patient, little one, your turn will come."

One by one, the little mermaid's sisters came of age, and visited the surface. They returned full of stories of all the things they had seen.

At last it was the turn of the little mermaid. She floated eagerly up towards the sea's surface.

When she finally pushed her face out through the salty swell,
she saw a fine ship floating nearby. The people were throwing a
party for the handsome prince on board.

The little mermaid couldn't take her eyes off the prince.

As she swam closer for a better look, a storm suddenly sprang
up and tossed the ship about on the huge waves.

The little mermaid watched in horror as the prince was
thrown into the churning sea. She dived down to rescue him.
Holding him in her arms, the little mermaid swam to shore and
gently pushed the unconscious prince onto the beach.

When she saw some people coming down the beach to help
the prince, she leaped back into the waves and swam home.

From that moment on, the little mermaid could think of
nothing but the prince and how she longed to be with him.

One day, when she couldn't bear it any longer, she visited the
evil sea witch.

"I can give you a potion to make you human, but I will take your beautiful voice in return," cackled the witch. "If you fail to win the prince's love, you will melt into sea foam and be gone forever!"

The little mermaid loved the prince so much that she agreed.

She swam to the shore and drank the potion, then fell into a deep sleep. When she woke up she was lying in the prince's palace. She tried to speak, but her voice was lost forever, and she could only smile at her handsome rescuer.

The prince was intrigued by the silent stranger. He took her everywhere and the little mermaid had never been happier.

Then, one day, the prince told her that he was to be married, but that he loved another girl, who had once rescued him from the sea. Without her voice, the little mermaid couldn't tell the prince that she was that girl.

On the day of the prince's wedding, the prince walked with the little mermaid along the beach. Suddenly, a huge wave crashed over the prince and the little mermaid, washing them out to sea. Without thinking, the little mermaid dived beneath the churning waves and grabbed the prince, taking him back to the shore.

"You're the girl who saved me before!" he cried.

The little mermaid smiled and nodded.

"I can't marry the princess. I love you," he sighed. "Will you marry me?" And as he kissed her, something magical happened. She could feel her voice returning!

"Yes!" she cried out with joy.

The couple were married the very next day. The little mermaid's dreams had come true, but she never forgot her family, or that she had once been a mermaid.

Elsie's Aeroplane

Elsie was a pilot. Her little aeroplane was very old and quite slow, but Elsie didn't care. She loved flying it up into the bright blue sky.

One sunny day, Elsie hurried to the airfield where her little aeroplane lived. She and her friends were going to have a race in their different kinds of flying machine. One friend flew an airliner, another had a seaplane, the third had a rocket and the last one had a jet. Each of them thought that they would be the fastest.

"Your slow, old aeroplane will come last," her friends said. But Elsie felt sure that her little aeroplane could do anything.

Elsie topped up the fuel and climbed into the cockpit. The five flying machines took off together, but they didn't stay together for long. The jet zoomed ahead. The airliner climbed high into the sky, and the rocket zigzagged around as if it were playing tag. Even the seaplane was going faster than Elsie.

"Don't worry," said Elsie, patting her little aeroplane. "I believe in you."

Suddenly, Elsie saw the airliner turn around and head back to the airfield.

"I forgot to top up on fuel," said the pilot into his crackly radio.

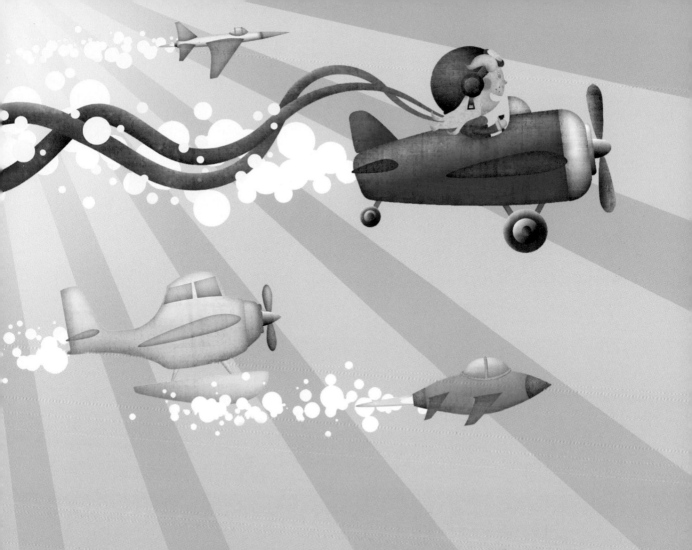

Then the jet zoomed off in the wrong direction. Elsie tried to tell him, but he was going too fast to listen.

The rocket flew higher and higher…and ended up in space!

"Only us left now!" said the pilot of the seaplane.

But just then, the pilot saw a lake and couldn't resist practising a water landing.

With a cheer, Elsie guided her little aeroplane over the finish line and won the race.

"We did it!" she cried. "Three cheers for the oldest, best little aeroplane in the world!"

The Big Freeze

It had been snowing all day, but when evening came, the flakes finally stopped falling. The forest was covered in a crisp, white blanket, and Scarlett the fox felt excited.

"I'll go for a walk to see how the forest looks," she said.

It was cold and the snow came almost to the top of her legs. She loved the crunching sound it made, and the way that the whole world seemed quieter.

Soon, Scarlett spotted some birds swooping and twittering high above.

"Good evening," she called. "Isn't the snow wonderful?"

"Exciting! Exciting!" the birds chirruped. "Never seen anything like it before! Amazing! Incredible! Are you going there now?"

"Going where?" Scarlett asked. But the birds were too excited to listen. They whirled and dived and looped the loop, staying high above and far ahead.

Scarlett walked on and saw her friend Rhys the owl. He was sitting on a high tree branch, hooting to his family.

"Come on," he called. "Hurry up! I don't want to miss a moment." He looked down and spotted Scarlett.

"Hello, Scarlett. What a night! What fun!"

"Hello," Scarlett replied. "I'm going for a walk to enjoy the snow. Would you like to join me?"

Rhys jumped up and down on his branch.

"Snow?" he cried. "Never mind the snow... There's something far more exciting to go and see!"

Suddenly, the owl's whole family started pushing out of the hole in the tree where they lived. Rhys was hidden among a flurry of soft feathers and excited hoots. Then the owls rose into the air and flew away.

"I wonder what he meant," thought Scarlett.
"Everyone is being very strange this evening!" She
started to walk faster, while overhead more and more birds
were flying in the same direction. Then she heard voices and
noticed a family of squirrels jumping around in the snow.

"It's magical!" one of them was shouting. "Amazing! We have
to go back." Snow puffed up around the squirrels as they
leaped up and down. Scarlett ran towards them to ask what was
happening, but they bounded away, giggling and chattering.
Scarlett chased after them. She had to find out what was
making everyone so happy.

As she ran, she saw more woodland creatures fluttering and
scurrying along. Even the daytime animals were there. It was as
if everyone who lived in the forest knew what was going on –
except Scarlett.

She stopped for a moment to catch her breath.

"That's strange," she said, panting. "We're heading towards the
river, but I can't hear the water babbling and splashing along
like normal."

She ran on, and when she came to the river, she understood.
It had frozen over like a skating rink! All the animals of the
forest had gathered there for a big skating party.

   As the sun went
down, the animals fluffed
up their fur and feathers. They shared
their food and helped each other onto the ice.
Scarlett wasn't very good at skating at first. Her legs kept
going in opposite directions. But Rhys hovered overhead, giving
her instructions, and the other animals stayed beside her until
she was spinning and twirling across the ice.

   All too soon, it was time to leave. Most of the animals had
already gone home, but Scarlett didn't want to go. She'd had so
much fun, she never wanted it to end.

   "I won't forget the Big Freeze," she thought as she watched
two ducks sliding around the rink. "I hope the snow will stay
another night, so I can do it all again." (And it did.)

Hoppity Rabbit's Big Adventure

Hoppity Rabbit lived in a beautiful meadow at the edge of the woods. He spent his days happily running and jumping and hopping through the tall grass, chasing butterflies and playing hide-and-seek with his best friend Boppity Rabbit.

On the other side of the meadow was a large stream. Hoppity loved to watch the fish darting about through the clear, flowing water, travelling on their journey towards the sea.

"I wonder what the sea is like?" Hoppity sighed, as he stared at the fish.

"Why don't we go on an adventure to find out?" said Boppity. "Look! The fish are swimming that way. If we follow the stream in the same direction, it should lead us to the sea."

Hoppity grinned. He'd never left the meadow or been on an adventure before.

"Let's pretend we're two fish racing to the sea!" Hoppity shouted, and dashed after Boppity along the grassy bank.

16

After a while, the grass stopped. A long, sandy beach stretched before them. The two little rabbits couldn't believe their eyes. The golden sand was covered in endless treasures of coloured shells and pebbles, curling seaweed and little scuttling crabs.

Hoppity grabbed Boppity's paw and turned to stare at the sea.

"It's even better than I imagined!" he cried, as the waves gently lapped at his feet. "Thank you, Boppity. This is the best adventure ever!"

Alice's Holiday

Alice was so excited about going on holiday! She hopped up and down by the door while Mum checked the locks and Dad looked for his flip-flops.

"Please hurry up!" cried Alice.

It took hours to drive to the airport. Then they had to check in, queue up, show their passports and wait as the luggage was loaded onto the aeroplane.

"Too much waiting!" cried Alice.

On the aeroplane, Alice talked to Mum and Dad until they fell asleep. Then she talked to herself. "I'm too excited to sleep!" she said.

When the aeroplane landed, they had to wait for their luggage, queue up, show their passports and wait for a taxi. Alice gave a big, BIG yawn.

In the hotel room, Mum and Dad unpacked and changed into their swimming costumes while Alice rested her eyes.

"Beach time!" said Mum. But Alice had fallen asleep!

Beach Penguin

Theo the penguin loved his snowy home. He loved jumping off icebergs and swimming races with his best friend Sophie. But, one night, his iceberg home floated away into warmer water and melted. When Theo woke up, he was near a beach!

"This place is amazing!" he said, waddling onto the sand.

Theo sunbathed in a stripy deckchair. He built a huge sandcastle. He hired a surfboard and rode the waves. He caught some tiny fish in the rock pools. He even had an ice cream!

Then, when his flippers were sandy and he was getting tired, he spotted a ship heading towards his home.

"Time to hitch a lift!" said Theo, diving into the warm water.

He couldn't wait to tell Sophie about his travels – and plan his next beach adventure!

Adventure Balloon

Eloise raced across the hill, panting and giggling.

"You can't catch me!" she yelled.

Her little brother Hal was behind her, running as fast as he could. Scruffy, their dog, barked and yapped as he bounded along beside Hal.

Suddenly, they saw a big basket sitting at the top of the hill. A huge hot-air balloon was attached to it, bobbing around in the breeze.

"It's beautiful!" said Eloise. "Let's go for a ride!"

"Hurrah! An adventure!" said Hal. "Come on, Scruffy. Let's go!"

Eloise hopped inside the basket, followed by Scruffy. Hal clambered in after them and then, magically, the balloon began to rise into the sky. They floated up among the fluffy white clouds. Birds fluttered around them, twittering with curiosity. The green hills and tall trees seemed small and far away. Scruffy barked and wagged his tail.

"Where shall we go?" Eloise called to the birds.

They cheeped even louder, but the children couldn't understand them. The balloon floated far over the land and, soon, they saw a rainbow-coloured tent in a green field.

"The circus!" Hal cried, clapping his hands. "I want to go to the circus!"

At once, the balloon floated down from the sky, heading towards the field.

As it got closer, clowns, jugglers and dancers came out of the tent. "Come and join our show!" they called out.

As soon as the balloon landed, Eloise, Hal and Scruffy raced inside the tent. It was lit by sparkling stars, and colourful balloons floated down to a huge crowd.

"Let the show begin!" cried a clown on stilts.

Scruffy did flips and somersaults on the back of a white horse, while Hal tiptoed across the tightrope.

Eloise stepped onto the circus swings, thinking of the birds that had flown around the balloon.

"I want to fly like the birds," she whispered.

Then she flew from swing to swing in the high roof of the tent, ever faster and higher. The crowd went wild.

Later, at the end of the show, the top of the circus tent opened like a lid. Everyone looked up. The hot-air balloon was floating above them.

"It's time to go!" Eloise told Hal and Scruffy.

They climbed into the basket and waved to the crowds and all the circus people below.

Then the balloon rose up into the clouds again. Eloise, Hal and Scruffy clung to the basket tightly as they soared with the birds, bees and butterflies.

Suddenly, the wind died down.

"Look!" said Eloise, peering over the edge of the basket. "We're back on the hill again."

Gently, the balloon bumped down onto the soft grass, and they all tumbled out. They lay on their backs, looking up at the blue sky.

"That was amazing," said Hal.

"WOOF!" said Scruffy.

"What an adventure!" said Eloise.

She laughed as the balloon seemed to give a little hop of excitement.

"See? The balloon thinks so too," she added with a giggle. "Come on, let's go home."

Verity's Fairy Tale

Verity's family lived in a castle. Verity loved living there, as her favourite books were all about handsome princes and beautiful princesses.

Verity even hoped that, one day, a prince would visit her castle and they would have an amazing adventure together, just like in her fairy-tale books. If only her prince would hurry up!

One day, Verity was peering out of the window in the highest tower, when she heard a rumbling noise.

"The steps!" she cried. "They're collapsing!"

The winding staircase fell away, and Verity was stuck.

"How will I get down now?" she thought.

Verity looked out of the window again, but not a single prince was galloping to her rescue on a white horse. All she could see was her little brother playing football in the garden.

"There's only one thing for it," Verity said. "I'll have to rescue myself."

Thinking quickly, Verity made a ladder out of some ivy vines that were clinging to the wall outside. Then she attached them to a hook inside the tower, and climbed down through the space where the steps used to be.

Down, down, down she went, and her ivy ladder spun and swung, but she hung on tight.

At last, Verity reached the bottom of the tower.

"I did it!" she cheered. "I rescued myself!"

And from that day on, Verity stopped waiting to have an adventure with a handsome prince. Instead, she went ahead and had them all on her own!

As Quiet As a...

Tabitha Mouse was trying to sleep. But every time she closed her eyes, she heard, "CAW! CAW!" It was very loud, and it was keeping her awake. She sat up and peeped out of her window. There were seven crows sitting in a row on a telephone wire. She opened her window and leaned out.

"Excuse me, crows," she said. "Could you be a bit quieter? I'm trying to sleep." But the crows just stared at her and said, "CAW" even more loudly.

"Oh dear," said Tabitha, wondering how she could get them to understand. She put one of her tiny fingers up to her mouth and said, "Shhh! As quiet as a whisper."

The crows hunched up their shoulders and tried their best. "CSHHHHAW! CSHHHHAW!" Tabitha put her paws over her ears. It was even louder than before! She thought again, then smiled. Tapping her head, she said, "As quiet as a thought."

The crows looked at each other and shrugged. They didn't know what she meant. They all started to caw more loudly than ever, wondering what the little mouse was saying.

"No, no," said Tabitha with a sigh.

Just then, she had an idea. She scurried outside and stood on the pavement underneath the crows. She waited for them to see her, then she raised her hands to signal for them to pay attention. When they were all watching, she rose up on her tiptoes and ran up and down in front of them. Suddenly, the crows understood. Tabitha was being 'as quiet as a mouse'!

The crows shut their beaks and didn't say another word. Tabitha went back to her room, took off her dressing gown and crept into bed. She peeped through the curtains at the crows, who had tucked their heads under their wings.

"Goodnight," said Tabitha, and she lay down and fell fast asleep.

The Best Zoo Ever!

Zoe the zookeeper had just finished doing her last rounds of the day to check on the animals. Normally at this time the zoo would be noisy with happy squawks, growls, splashes and toots. But not tonight. Silence had replaced the usual animal chatter.

"What's wrong?" Zoe asked the big grey rhinoceros, as she passed his enclosure on her way to the main gates. "Why is everyone so quiet?"

"We're bored," said the rhinoceros. "Nothing exciting ever happens here."

Zoe didn't want the animals to be unhappy. What could she do to cheer them up?

That night, as she lay in bed, Zoe suddenly had a great idea. She decided to call some of her friends in the morning to see if they could help her put it into action.

All of the following week, the zoo was noisy with the sound of hammering and sawing, digging and drilling. The animals looked on curiously as Zoe and her friends rushed around, wearing hard hats and tool belts, and carrying planks of wood and plastic pipes.

At last, the project was finished. Zoe called all the animals together. They couldn't believe their eyes! There, in the middle of the zoo, was the most amazing adventure play area.

"I hope this will stop you from being bored," said Zoe. "I declare this zoo-tastic park open!"

And for the rest of that day the animals played hide-and-seek in the trees and bushes. They slithered down the slide and swung from the bars of the jungle gym.

That evening, as Zoe settled the animals back into their enclosures, she smiled at all their happy faces.

"Thank you so much, Zoe!" cried the big grey rhinoceros. "We had so much fun today. This really is the best zoo ever!"

A New Friend

Octopus loved playing with her friends Dolphin and Turtle. Every morning, they played a game called 'Sharks' by the old shipwreck near Octopus's cave. In the game, one of the friends would be the shark, while the other two swam away, pretending to be scared.

One morning, Dolphin and Turtle went to meet Octopus, but she wasn't in her cave.

"Where is she?" asked Dolphin, anxiously. "Octopus always waits for us here…"

"Perhaps she's in trouble and needs our help," cried Turtle.

As the two friends set off to find Octopus, they bumped into…a shark!

"Go away!" squeaked Dolphin, shaking with fear.

"Please don't eat us," begged Turtle, starting to cry.

The shark smiled sadly. "I don't want to eat you. I just want to be friends."

He sounded so unhappy that both Turtle and Dolphin felt sorry for him.

"Well," said Turtle, nervously, "maybe you can help us find our friend Octopus."

Shark groaned. "Octopus? Oh, no! I think I scared her away from that cave…"

Turtle and Dolphin glanced at each other. They knew exactly where Octopus would be…at the shipwreck waiting for them! So they swam as fast as they could, with Shark trailing behind.

There, in the wreck, was Octopus. She was tangled in an old fishing net.

Turtle and Dolphin tried to undo the knots but soon their flippers and fins were tangled too.

"Let me help," said Shark. He bit a huge hole in the net with his sharp teeth and set the three friends free.

"Thank you, Shark," said Turtle.

"You saved our lives," gasped Dolphin.

"I'm sorry we were frightened of you," added Octopus, shyly.

Shark smiled. "Can we be friends now?"

"Oh, yes, please," beamed Turtle. "Come on, let's play."

"But not 'Sharks'," laughed Dolphin, looking at Shark. "Maybe you can teach us a new game."

31

Sophie's Smile

All the other fish were afraid of Sophie. "She's always frowning," they said. "Why does she look so grumpy?" But poor Sophie wasn't really cross. That was just the shape of her mouth. She couldn't seem to smile and look friendly.

One day, Sophie had an idea.

"I'll throw a party," she said. "I'll show them that they don't have to be scared of me." She spent a long time getting everything ready. She sent out her invitations on tiny shells, and decorated a cave with coral in every colour she could find. She arranged for the most famous underwater band in the sea to be there, and she lit the cave with tiny crystal jellyfish.

The guests arrived and swam shyly into the cave. They looked nervous when they said hello, and Sophie's heart sank. If only they could see that she was kind and happy! But she nodded to the band, and they began to play.

"Come and dance!" she called.

One by one, the other fish started to dance. Sophie stayed back because she didn't want to frighten anyone. But as the dancers swirled faster and faster, they saw that Sophie wasn't scary at all. She was nervous, just like them!

The whirlpool of dancing fish spun Sophie, sending her topsy-turvy. She twirled around so fast that everything about her got turned upside down…including her frown!

When the music stopped playing, and everyone stopped dancing, the other fish gathered around Sophie. They were all smiling now they knew that Sophie was so friendly. And when they looked at her, they saw that something about her had changed too. Now she was wearing a big, happy smile!

33

Little Dragon and the Birthday Surprise

Little Dragon was playing with Princess Pippa, Prince Pip and Baron Boris.

"It's great to have a real dragon for a friend!" said Pip.

"He's not a real dragon!" said Boris. "He can't breathe fire!"

"Yes, I can!" said Little Dragon angrily.

"Go on, Little Dragon, show him!" said Pippa.

Little Dragon tried…and tried… and tried! But nothing happened.

"Liar, liar, you can't breathe fire!" sang Boris.

Little Dragon felt weary, teary and miserable.

"Never mind!" said Pippa. "I'm sure you'll be able to breathe fire when you're older."

"But when will I be older?" asked Little Dragon.

"On your birthday, of course!" said Pip.

"What's a birthday?" asked Little Dragon.

"You have them every year on the day that you were born," said Pip.

"But I wasn't born," sniffed Little Dragon. "I hatched!"

"When?" asked Pippa and Pip together.

"I don't know!" cried Little Dragon. "I was too little to tell the time!" He started to cry.

"Well," said Pippa, "if you haven't had a birthday yet, then it's about time you did! Tomorrow can be your birthday and we'll have a party with balloons, ice cream and games – and a big birthday cake with candles on the top!"

And that's exactly what they did. It was a wonderful party!

There was music and dancing, funny games to play, lots of yummy things to eat, and a pile of presents for Little Dragon!

Then the magic wagon brought in the birthday cake and everyone sang, "Happy birthday to you!"

"Oh, no!" cried Princess Pippa. "Who will light the candles! How can Little Dragon blow them out and make a wish?"

"Don't worry," said Little Dragon. "I'll blow on them anyway, just for luck!"

He took a big breath, then…Little Dragon's birthday wish came true! His fiery breath lit all the candles in one go!

Baron Boris was a bit scared, but everybody else cheered.

"Yippee!" shouted Little Dragon. "I do like birthdays!"

Mermaid's Treasure

One morning, Pearl the mermaid was playing around a reef when she spotted a large sea chest among the coral. She swam closer.

"It must have fallen out of a ship," she exclaimed. "I wonder what's inside!"

But when she tried to lift the lid, she found that it was locked.

"Oh, bother," Pearl muttered. "Now I want to look inside even more!"

She tried to force the lid open with a clam shell, but it wouldn't budge. So she asked her biggest, strongest friends for help.

Shark tried to bite a hole in it. Octopus wrapped his tentacles around the chest and tried to squeeze it open. Whale tried crushing it with his weight.

"It's no use," sighed Pearl. "We'll never get it open."

"May I try?" said a squeaky voice in her ear.

Pearl turned and saw a tiny shrimp, no bigger than her fingernail. She smiled at him. How could someone so small open the chest?

"Of course you may," she said politely.

The little shrimp wriggled through the keyhole. Pearl, Shark, Octopus and Whale watched as he reached into the lock with his spindly legs. Then there was a loud click, and the chest unlocked.

The shrimp swam out, looking very pleased with himself.

"Well done!" cried Pearl.

Slowly, she lifted the lid. The chest was full of men's clothes! Pearl sat back and laughed loudly.

"Some poor sailor has lost his luggage," she chuckled. "I suppose it would be treasure to him!"

She looked at her friends and laughed again.

"Don't look so disappointed," she went on. "We may not have gold or jewels, but we've made a very clever friend."

And the little pink shrimp blushed bright red!

37

The Dinosaur Marching Band

One, two, three, four! Keep it up, two, three, four!
The jungle rumbles and the ground shakes.
CRASH! THUMP! What's that sound?

Oh, look! It's the dinosaur marching band, and they're coming this way! Crashing, stomping, singing and playing their loud music as they sway through the trees.

STOMP! STOMP! TOOT! TOOT! BANG! BANG!

What an impressive noise they make!

Tommy T. Rex is at the head of the line. He leads his fellow musical marchers, tooting loudly on his golden trumpet, the melody floating on the air.

Following closely behind is Daisy Diplodocus. With a steady beat on her jungle drums, she sways her long neck and stamps her large feet, keeping the rhythm for the rest of the band.

Susie Stegosaurus sings her sweet, soulful song, hitting the high notes perfectly. LA, LA, LA, LA, LA!

Then there's Terry Pterodactyl, flying above his marching friends. He whistles the melody with Tommy's crisp trumpet notes, while Arthur Ankylosaurus hammers a bass beat on the ground in time with Daisy's drums.

And, last but not least, Trixie Triceratops stomps along at the back of the line, keeping time as she counts: "One, two, three, four! Keep it up, two, three, four!" She shouts out the numbers with a noisy ROAR!

STOMP! STOMP! TOOT! TOOT! BANG! BANG!

It's the wonderful musical dinosaur marching band… and they're coming your way.

The Curious Star

Once upon a time there was a curious star that wanted to know what humans were really like. So, one night, he let go of the sky and fell all the way down to Earth. When he landed, he plopped into a muddy puddle next to a pigsty.

"Hello," said the star to a round, pink creature. "Are you a human?"

"No," chuckled the pig. "Humans are much taller than me!"

So the star went shooting through the sky until he spotted a tall creature with a very long neck.

"Hello," said the star. "Are you a human?"

"No," smiled the giraffe. "Humans only have two legs. I have four."

The star sighed. He was longing to meet a real human. He zoomed on until he spotted someone standing on two legs and squawking.

"Hello," said the star. "Are you a human?"

"Certainly not!" said the parrot. "Humans aren't as bright and beautiful as I am!"

"Oh dear," said the star. "Perhaps I'll never meet a human."

When the sun came up, he flew down to a sandy beach to rest. Before long, a creature with curious eyes and messy hair kneeled down beside him.

"Hello," said the star. "Are you a human?"

"Yes, I am," laughed the little boy. "My name's Noah. Would you like to play with me?"

The star jumped up in excitement. Together they explored rock pools, made sandcastles, and played hide-and-seek all day. And the star found out that Noah was very, very curious – just like him!

When night fell, the curious star said goodbye to Noah.

"Don't stop being curious," he said. "Exploring new things can take you to amazing places."

With a blast of silver light, the star shot into the air and took his place again in the twinkling night sky.

The Enchanted Garden

Princess Sylvie loved to walk through the meadows to look at the flowers.

One day, she found an overgrown path in her favourite meadow. She asked a woman where the path led.

"To the garden of the enchantress!" said the woman. "You can go and look, but they say that whatever you do, don't pick the flowers."

Princess Sylvie followed the path until she came to a cottage with the prettiest garden she had ever seen, filled with flowers of every colour and perfume.

Princess Sylvie went back to the garden every day.

Soon she forgot all about the enchantress, and one day, she picked a rose from the garden and took it back to the castle. As she put it in water, Princess Sylvie suddenly remembered the warning!

But months passed and nothing happened. The rose stayed as fresh as the day it was picked. Forgetting her fears, Princess Sylvie went back to the enchanted garden.

But when she saw the garden, Princess Sylvie wanted to cry. The grass was brown. All the flowers had withered.

Then she heard someone weeping. Inside the cottage, the enchantress was sitting by the fire, crying. She was old and bent. Princess Sylvie was afraid, but she felt sorry for her.

"What happened to your lovely garden?" Princess Sylvie asked.

"Someone picked a rose from it!" said the enchantress. "The garden is under a spell. The picked flower will live forever, but the rest of the flowers must die! And when the rose was picked, my magic was lost, too, and I too am beginning to wither and die!"

"What can I do?" said Princess Sylvie.

"Only a princess can help," the enchantress replied. "She must bring me six sacks of stinging nettles! And no princess would do that!"

Princess Sylvie gathered six sacks of nettles, not caring that they stung her, and took them back to the enchantress.

The enchantress said, "But the nettles must be picked by a princess."

"I am a princess," said Princess Sylvie.

The enchantress made a magic potion with the nettles and drank it. Instantly, the garden became beautiful again. Princess Sylvie gasped! Gone was the bent old lady. In her place was a beautiful young woman.

"My garden is restored," smiled the enchantress, "and so am I!"

And so the enchantress and the princess became great friends and shared the enchanted garden.

Ollie's Adventure

One day, Ollie the dolphin was playing in the deep, bubbly ocean. His mum was nearby, but he was busy doing somersaults, twirls and loops. Then, all of a sudden, Ollie was alone. He couldn't see his mum anywhere.

"Mum!" he called. "Where are you?" The ocean suddenly seemed very big.

Soon, Ollie saw a crab scuttling along the seabed.

"Will you help me find my mum?" Ollie asked.

The crab clicked his pincers. "I'm too busy to look for dolphins," he snapped, so Ollie swam on.

After a while, Ollie came to a big underwater cave. An octopus floated out towards him.

"Have you seen my mum?" Ollie asked.

The octopus shook his head.

"Ask the jellyfish," he said. But the glowing jellyfish just shrugged, then opened and closed like an umbrella.

"Oh dear," said Ollie. "How am I ever going to find my way home?"

Then, suddenly, Ollie remembered something.

"If you ever get lost, I will wait for you next to the big shipwreck," his mum had told him.

Ollie darted after the jellyfish. "Which way is the big shipwreck?" he asked.

This time, the jellyfish knew the answer. "I'll light the way!" she said.

As they passed the cave, Ollie called out to the octopus, "We're on the way to the shipwreck!"

"I know where that is!" boomed the octopus. He used his tentacles to point the way.

Even the crab helped to lead Ollie to the big shipwreck. And there beside it was…

"Mum!" Ollie darted towards her and they rubbed noses.

"I'm so happy you remembered our meeting place," said Ollie's mum.

"Me too," said Ollie. "And now I know my way here, I will never get lost again!"

The Greedy Pup

Mr and Mrs Dog were very busy animals. They had five puppies to look after! Chocolate and Coffee had brown spots, Sunny and Daffodil had yellow spots, and Custard was yellow all over.

Custard's brothers and sisters were always being called 'good dog'. They never barked too loudly or chewed up slippers. They never jumped on the sofa or got mud on their collars.

But Custard was always up to mischief…especially when it came to food. If there were snacks to be found, then you could be sure that Custard would find them.

One morning, the Dog family were eating their breakfast together. Chocolate and Sunny had a friendly tug of war, while Daffodil and Coffee gnawed on their bones. Custard, who had already finished his bone, saw that no one was looking and drank everyone else's milk. His tummy gave a loud rumble.

"Was that thunder?" asked Mr Dog.

"Where has all the milk gone?" asked Mrs Dog.

Custard thought that this was a good time to go for a walk. He was still hungry after breakfast, and he was very good at finding a few extra titbits to keep him going until lunchtime.

First, he visited the hot dog stand at the end of the road. He rose up on his hind legs and panted. The man selling hot dogs grinned at him.

"All right, you cheeky pup," he said. "Have a hot dog!" He flipped a hot dog into a bun and smothered it in tomato sauce. Then he sent it spinning through the air, and Custard caught it and ate it up in three gulps.

But Custard was still hungry, so he ran down to the ice-cream stall. The ice-cream seller was busily mixing different flavours.

"Hello, Custard!" she exclaimed. "Will you help me taste some new flavours?"

Custard could hardly wait. He tried mint and raspberry, and caramel and banana, but his favourite was apple and cinnamon. He had three scoops, a cone and a flake.

Next, Custard visited his friend Patch's café. All the customers smiled when they saw him licking his lips. One shared their toast with him, another gave him some scrambled egg, while a third handed him a plate of baked beans, sausages and grilled tomatoes. Custard wolfed it all down.

Soon, Custard started to make his way home. He was beginning to feel a bit full.

The ginger cat on his street had a bowl of cat treats outside her house. She offered some to Custard. He tried one, but he didn't like it at all.

"Now I feel really full," he thought.

The dog on the corner had a bowl full of delicious-looking biscuits, but Custard didn't ask to share it. He padded by without even as much as a sniff.

Custard was almost home when he spotted a large cake sitting on the doorstep outside his house. It had yellow icing with white flowers all over it. Custard looked around, but no one seemed to own it.

"It wouldn't be fair to leave this cake here on its own," he said. "Cakes are meant to be eaten. Even if I don't want it, I know my family will!"

He carefully picked up the plate in his teeth and took it inside. His mother was waiting for him.

"Custard, you naughty pup," she started to say. Then she stopped and looked at the cake he was carrying.

"You found it!" she cried. "I couldn't remember where I'd put it. We were going to surprise you with it after breakfast!"

Custard put the plate down and saw the writing on the top: "HAPPY BIRTHDAY, CUSTARD!"

"I forgot it was my birthday!" he said. "Thanks, everyone."

But Custard was still not feeling hungry. So he let his family tuck into the cake.

Barking and cheering, his brothers and sisters bounded over. Soon the whole cake had disappeared. Then they snuggled up together and snoozed in the family basket.

Custard smiled in his sleep. He didn't mind about not eating his birthday cake…he knew a lovely bakery around the corner. He might visit it tomorrow!

Mother Hulda

There was once a woman with two daughters. Her stepdaughter was hard-working, while her own daughter was lazy. The woman preferred her birth daughter, and made her stepdaughter do all the work around the house.

One day, the woman gave her stepdaughter an enormous basket of wool.

"Take this wool and spin it all. Don't come back until it's finished," she told her stepdaughter.

So the stepdaughter sat and spun until her fingers bled. Just as she lowered a bucket into the well, ready to scoop up some water to wash her fingers, she accidentally dropped the spindle. It fell into the water at the bottom of the well with a PLOP!

The girl climbed down to find the spindle and, at the bottom of the well, she found herself in a strange land with orange trees, blue grass and a pink sky.

After a while, she reached a little house. A kind woman called Mother Hulda lived there. She gave the girl food and shelter. In return, the girl helped Mother Hulda with all her chores.

Even though Mother Hulda was kinder than her stepmother, the girl began to feel homesick.

"I would like to return home," said the girl.

So Mother Hulda gave the girl back her spindle and, as the girl left the strange land, a shower of gold coins fell at her feet.

When the girl arrived home with the coins, her stepmother was amazed. She wanted the same thing to happen to her own lazy daughter.

"Do just as your sister did," she told the idle girl.

But the stepmother's daughter could not be bothered to sit and spin, so she stuck her hands into a thorny bush to make them bleed. Then she dropped the spindle down the well and climbed in after it.

The girl knocked on Mother Hulda's door, asking for food and shelter. After eating, she fell asleep, snoring like a pig!

"Give me back my spindle. I want to go home now," said the rude girl to Mother Hulda when she woke up.

So Mother Hulda took the girl back to the bottom of the well. But instead of gold coins, it was tar that fell at her feet.

The girl returned to her mother, who tried to scrub her shoes clean. But the tar was stuck fast, and has remained there ever since.

How the Cardinal Bird Got His Colour

Once upon a time, there was a raccoon who loved to tease his neighbour, the wolf. The raccoon would pull the wolf's tail, then run away, hide up a tree, and drop pine cones on the wolf's head. And when the wolf was asleep he would tickle his nose with a feather until he sneezed.

One day the wolf got so angry with the raccoon that he chased him through the forest. When the raccoon reached the river, he climbed up into the branches of a tall tree and waited to see what the wolf would do.

The wolf saw the raccoon's reflection in the water, so he jumped into the river to catch him. But the raccoon had disappeared!

"He must be under the water," thought the wolf, diving down to search the riverbed.

Finally, exhausted from his efforts, the wolf climbed onto the bank and fell into a deep sleep.

As soon as the wolf was snoring, the raccoon came down from the tree to play yet another trick on the poor wolf. He got some mud from the river and stuck it all over the wolf's eyes. When the wolf woke up, he couldn't open his eyes.

"Help!" he cried. "I can't see! I've gone blind!" A brown bird, who was perched in the branches of the tree, took pity on the wolf.

"I am just a little brown bird," he said. "Everyone says that I am very dull and boring, but I will help you if I can."

The bird flew down and carefully picked the dried mud from the wolf's eyes until he could open them.

"Thank you," said the wolf. "Now I would like to do something for you in return. Please follow me."

The wolf led the bird to a rock that oozed red dye. He took a twig and chewed it until the end was like a paintbrush, then he dipped it into the red dye and painted the brown bird's feathers a glorious red colour.

"From now on you will be known as the cardinal bird in honour of your beautiful red plumage," the wolf told him.

The bird was very proud of his colourful feathers – no one would ever call him dull and boring again.

And that is how the beautiful cardinal bird got his colour.

The Frog Prince

Long ago, a princess lived with her father in a palace surrounded by woods.

When it was hot outside, the princess would walk into the shade of the forest and sit by a pond. There she would play with her favourite toy, a golden ball.

One day, the ball slipped from her hand and fell to the bottom of the pond. "My beautiful golden ball," she sobbed.

An ugly, speckled frog popped his head out of the water. "Why are you crying?" he croaked.

"I've dropped my precious golden ball into the water," she cried.

"What will you give me if I get it for you?" asked the frog.

"You may have my jewels," sobbed the unhappy princess.

54

"I don't need those," said the frog. "If you promise to care for me and be my friend, let me share food from your plate and sleep on your pillow, then I will bring back your golden ball."

"I promise," said the princess, but she thought to herself, "He's only a silly old frog. I won't do any of those things."

When the frog returned with the ball, she snatched it from him and ran back to the palace.

That evening, the princess was having dinner with her father when there was a knock on the door.

When the princess opened the door, she was horrified to find the frog sitting there. She slammed the door and hurried back to the table.

"Who was that?" asked the king.

"Oh, just a frog," replied the princess.

"What does a frog want with you?" asked the puzzled king.

The princess told her father about the promise she had made.

"Princesses always keep their promises," insisted the king. "Let the frog in and make him welcome."

As soon as the frog hopped through the door he asked to be lifted up onto the princess's plate. When the frog saw the look of disgust on the princess's face, he sang:

"Princess, princess, fair and sweet, you made a special vow
To be my friend and share your food, so don't forget it now."

The king was annoyed to see his daughter acting so rudely. "This frog helped you," he said. "And now you must keep your promise to him."

For the rest of the day, the frog followed the princess everywhere she went. She hoped that he would go back to his pond when it was time for bed, but when darkness fell, the frog yawned and said, "I am tired. Take me to your room and let me sleep on your pillow."

The princess was horrified. "No, I won't!" she said rudely. "Go back to your pond and leave me alone!"

The patient frog sang:

"Princess, princess, fair and sweet, you made a special vow
To be my friend and share your food, so don't forget it now."

Reluctantly, the princess took the frog to her room. She couldn't bear the thought of sleeping next to him, so she put him on the floor. Then she climbed into her bed and went to sleep.

After a while, the frog jumped up onto the bed. "It's draughty on the floor. Let me sleep on your pillow," he said.

The sleepy princess felt more annoyed than ever. She picked up the frog and hurled him across the room. But when she saw him lying dazed and helpless on the floor, she was suddenly filled with pity.

"Oh, you poor darling!" she cried, and she picked him up and kissed him.

Suddenly, the frog transformed into a handsome young prince.

"Sweet princess," he cried. "I was bewitched and your tender kiss has broken the curse!"

The prince and princess soon fell in love and were married. They often walked in the shady forest together and sat by the pond, tossing the golden ball back and forth, and smiling at how they met.

The Enchanted Shell

Anna lived in a big, white house by the sea. She loved to watch the sun go down behind the waves and listen to the splashing of the surf.

One evening, she was walking along the beach when she saw a pearly pink shell lying on the sand.

"How pretty!" she said, picking up the shell. Suddenly, the shell started to sparkle. Then it rose into the air and flew into the sea, where it grew bigger and bigger, until it was the size of a small boat!

Anna climbed into the shell and it took her further and further out to sea.

The stars came out, and moonlight danced on the water. Fish in all the colours of the rainbow swirled around the shell, making it spin slowly. A purple octopus peeped over the side of the shell and smiled at Anna.

From beneath the water, music rose up. It was the most wonderful music that Anna had ever heard. Then a beautiful mermaid appeared.

"My sisters and I make music every night," said
the mermaid. "The octopus will look after your boat.
Come and play!"

Anna slipped into the water and the mermaid led her
to a glimmering blue-green palace under the sea. Mermaids
danced around Anna, their tails twinkling.

Anna stayed with the mermaids until the stars disappeared and
the sun came up. It was time to leave. Anna swam to the boat
and it carried her back to the beach by her home.

Walking home, Anna held tightly to the little shell. She knew
that more adventures would find her whenever she visited the
beach with the special shell in the moonlight!

Thumbelina

Once upon a time, there was a poor woman who lived all alone. She dreamed of having a child of her own with whom she could share her home. One day, she decided to visit a kindly witch who lived at the end of her lane to ask for help.

"Take this grain and plant it in a pot," said the witch. "Water it and care for it. The grain will do the rest."

Every morning the woman checked on her precious plant. Within a week, it had grown into a tall flower.

"I've never seen anything as beautiful," said the woman, bending down to give the bud a gentle kiss.

POP! The pink flower suddenly opened up its petals. Sitting inside it was a tiny girl, no bigger than the woman's thumb. The woman was overjoyed.

"I shall call you Thumbelina," she cried.

Thumbelina and her mother were very happy. Then, one night, while they slept, a warty toad took Thumbelina away.

"You will make the perfect wife for my son," hissed the toad, placing Thumbelina on a lily pad in the middle of a stream. Then the toad swam off to find her son.

Poor Thumbelina started to cry – she didn't want to marry a toad.

"Don't cry, little girl," said a passing fish. "I'll help you."

The kind fish nibbled through the stem of the lily pad and it floated free downstream. At last, it drifted to the riverbank, and Thumbelina jumped off.

All summer, Thumbelina lived happily among the flowers. But when winter arrived, she was cold and hungry.

A kind field mouse invited her to spend the winter in his cosy underground burrow. It was warm and snug, but Thumbelina missed the sunlight.

One day, the mouse's friend, a mole, asked Thumbelina to marry him. Thumbelina didn't want to marry the mole and live underground. But, as the mouse had been so kind to her, Thumbelina agreed to a wedding the following summer.

As the wedding day grew closer, Thumbelina became more sad. One morning, she was miserably wandering through the underground tunnels of the mouse's home, when she came across a swallow. He was almost dead with cold.

"I will help you," said Thumbelina, hugging the bird to her.

"Thank you," sighed the swallow, "you have saved my life. I will take you to a place where the sun always shines."

Tears ran down Thumbelina's cheeks. "I can't leave," she cried. "I have to marry Mole."

"I will never forget what you have done for me," said the swallow, and he left.

Summer came around again, and the day of Thumbelina's marriage to Mole. As Thumbelina stepped outside to say goodbye to the sunshine forever, the swallow swooped down.

"Quick, come with me!" he chirped. And this time Thumbelina didn't refuse.

The land of sunshine was full of beautiful flowers. As Thumbelina reached out to touch a pretty bud, its petals opened to reveal a tiny fairy prince.

All around her, little fairies appeared.
"Will you marry me?" asked the tiny prince.
"I will!" replied Thumbelina, grinning joyfully.
She knew she had found the place where she
truly belonged.

The Peacock's Complaint

Peacock was very unhappy about his ugly voice, and he spent most of his days complaining about it to anyone who would listen.

One day, Fox had had enough of Peacock's constant moaning.

"It is true that you cannot sing," he said, "but look how beautiful you are. Your feathers are amazing!"

Peacock looked at his feathers.

"Oh, what good is all this beauty," he groaned, "if I have such an unpleasant voice?"

Fox sighed. "Everyone has their own special gift. You have your beauty, the nightingale has his song, the owl has his eyes and the eagle has his strength."

But Peacock continued to moan.

"Even if you had a musical voice," Fox shouted in frustration, "you would find something else to complain about!"

And the moral of the story is: do not envy the gifts of others. Make the most of your own.

The Goose that Laid the Golden Eggs

A farmer and his wife owned a very special goose. Every day, the goose would lay a golden egg. The couple sold the eggs and, before long, they became rich.

The goose continued to lay her golden eggs and the farmer and his wife got richer and richer. But, sadly, they also became greedy. In spite of their great wealth, they were not satisfied.

One day, the farmer's wife turned to her husband and said, "Just think, if we could have all the golden eggs that are in this goose, we could be even richer, even more quickly!"

The farmer grinned at his wife.

"You're right," he cried. "We wouldn't have to wait for her to lay an egg every day."

So, the greedy couple killed the goose. Of course, she was like every other goose. She had no golden eggs inside her at all. And that was the end of the golden eggs!

And the moral of this story is: too much greed results in nothing.

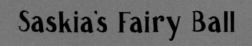

Saskia's Fairy Ball

Saskia the fairy was organising the fairy ball. But, on the morning of the ball, she lost her wand!

"How am I going to get everything ready for tonight without magic?" she cried.

Suddenly, she had an idea. She was good friends with the woodland animals, and she had been planning to invite them all. Perhaps they would help her!

First, Saskia had to find a place to hold the ball. Without her wand, she couldn't build a palace, so she chose a little clearing in the forest. Next, she visited the squirrels and rabbits, and explained her problem.

"Will you help me?" she asked. "I need food, decorations and music."

"We can make nut muffins," the squirrels squeaked.

"Carrot cupcakes!" the rabbits cried, hopping around.

Saskia flew up to the treetops to visit her magpie friends.

"You love sparkly things," she said. "Will you find decorations for the trees?"

The magpies agreed and flew off. Finally, Saskia asked the fireflies to light up the ball and the songbirds to provide the music.

At last, the sun went down and the stars began to
twinkle. Fireflies danced above the clearing, lighting
up the sparkling jewellery in the trees. Toadstool tables
were piled high with cupcakes and muffins.

"It's perfect," said Saskia, dancing around with her
animal friends. "Thank you so much for helping!"

The fairy guests arrived, expecting a castle and a
ballroom, but when they saw the clearing, they clapped
their hands in delight. The Fairy Queen stepped forward
and took Saskia by the hand.

"You have done magnificently," she said. "You've
made our animal friends part of the evening and
created a beautiful setting for the ball. From now on,
our balls shall always be outside!"

Little Dragon Goes Fishing

Little Dragon was fishing. He dipped his net in the pond and swished it around.

"I've caught a fish!" he cried. But he hadn't caught a fish at all. He had caught a red rubber boot.

"One boot is not much use on its own," said Little Dragon. "I need to catch the other one too."

He was just about to dip the net in the water again when along came his friends, Princess Pippa, Prince Pip and Baron Boris.

"What are you doing?" they asked.

"I'm catching red rubber boots," said Little Dragon. "Do you want to take a turn?"

"Yes, please!" said Princess Pippa. "I've always wanted a pair of red boots."

Princess Pippa swished the net around in the pond, and pulled out...a yellow umbrella.

"I wasn't expecting that!" she said.

Prince Pip took a turn with the fishing net too.

"I've caught something heavy!" he called. He heaved the net out of the water.

"It's...a blue bucket full of holes!"

Baron Boris grabbed the net.

"It's my turn now!" he said. "I'm going to catch something much better than that."

Baron Boris spotted something under a lily pad. "A green fish!" he cried. And he leaned forward to scoop it up.

Oh, dear! It wasn't a green fish at all. It was a green frog... and an angry one, too!

"Ribbet!" it croaked, leaping out of the net. Baron Boris was so scared that he fell into the water with a SPLASH!

"I think we will need a much bigger net to catch Baron Boris!" said Little Dragon.

The Lemur Dance

Louis the Lemur had a secret. He loved to dance, but none of the other lemurs knew, because Louis was very shy. He never went down to the river to play. He never joined in games of hide-and-seek. And when all the other lemurs decided to do a Lemur Dance, Louis would run away and hide.

One day, when the other lemurs were playing in the forest, Louis crept out from his hiding place and began to sway. He closed his eyes and began to twirl. He hummed, and then leaped into the air and spun around and around. He was having such a wonderful time that he didn't hear the other lemurs coming back. When he opened his eyes and saw them, he stopped dancing at once!

"Don't stop!" cried Melanie the Lemur, grabbing his paw. "You're a great dancer!"

"Wow," thought Louis, as they twirled around and around. "Dancing with other lemurs isn't at all scary. It's even better than dancing alone!"

After that, Louis always played and danced with the other lemurs. And he was never ever shy ever again.

SSSSHHH!

One morning Lion was very tired, so he curled up for a nap. He was just dozing off when Monkey began to screech.

"Ssssh!" roared Lion angrily. "Can't a lion get any peace?"

Monkey crept away.

Lion settled back down and closed his eyes. He was just beginning to snore when Elephant came stomping by.

"Ssssh!" roared Lion angrily. "Can't a lion get any peace?"

"Sorry," whispered Elephant, and he tiptoed away.

Suddenly there was a loud hiss. It was Snake passing by.

"Ssssh!" roared Lion angrily. "Can't a lion get any peace?"

"S…s…sorry," hissed Snake.

Lion closed his eyes again, but it was no use. No matter how hard he tried, he was much too angry by now to fall asleep.

"What you need is a jungle lullaby," squeaked a little mouse. "Listen to the whispering breeze, and the stream bubbling down to the waterhole. Listen to the crickets singing in the grass. That's a jungle lullaby! Can you hear it?"

But Lion never said a word. He was fast asleep. Ssssh!

The Nightingale

A long, long time ago, Ancient China was ruled by a rich and proud emperor. The emperor loved to be surrounded by fine, expensive objects. The more they glittered with jewels and gold, the happier he was. He had a magnificent palace, filled with priceless treasures, which overlooked the most exquisite gardens.

Talk of the emperor's spectacular palace and gardens spread far and wide. Its beauty was held in such high esteem that many people wrote stories about it. The emperor liked to entertain himself by reading these books. He would sit in his throne room, nodding his approval at each new line of praise. He was a very happy man – until the day he read something that filled his proud heart with jealousy!

In the forest, beyond the emperor's gardens, there lived a tiny brown nightingale. The nightingale loved to sing. Every evening it would warble melodies so beautiful, they filled the heart with happiness.

The emperor hadn't even known of the nightingale's existence or the matchless beauty of its song until that moment.

"Get me the bird! I must hear it sing! How can anything be more beautiful than my palace?" screamed the emperor.

His lord-in-waiting hurried off to find the nightingale.

"Little bird, please come and sing for the emperor," he said.

"It would be an honour," chirped the tiny bird.

Back at the palace, the nightingale sang its glorious song. The tenderness of the melody touched the emperor's heart.

"You must stay and sing for me every day," he cried.

Day after day, the tiny bird sang its magnificent melodies for the emperor. It never complained about being kept in a cage, but it grew sad because it missed the freedom of its forest home.

Then, one day, the emperor received a gift. It was a clockwork nightingale made out of gold and jewels. Its song was beautiful, and the emperor loved his new toy so much that he lost interest in the real nightingale. The little nightingale escaped and flew back to its forest home.

A year went by, and the emperor played his mechanical bird day and night, until finally the toy broke. The emperor was devastated. Now he had no bird to sing to him. He was filled with sadness.

Day after day, he grew weaker and weaker. Then, one evening, as the emperor lay in his bed, close to death, a blissful harmony suddenly floated in through his open window. It was the nightingale.

"You came back," whispered the emperor. He felt comfort in his heart, and his fever disappeared. "I do not deserve your sweet music. How can I ever repay you?"

"I don't want anything," replied the nightingale. "Knowing that I have touched your heart is enough. I can't come and live in your palace, but I will visit you every evening."

The emperor's face filled with happiness. He realised how foolish and empty his love of riches was. He had been given a second chance, and he vowed to rule his empire wisely from then on.

How the Bear Lost His Tail

Once upon a time, the bear had a long tail, and the fox was very jealous of it.

"What makes Bear think his tail is so wonderful?" growled the fox, as he looked at his own splendid russet-coloured tail. "My tail is much finer than his. I'm going to teach him a lesson."

It was winter, and all the lakes were covered with thick ice. The fox made a hole in the ice and surrounded it with fat, tasty-looking fish. That evening, when the bear passed by, the fox dangled his tail through the hole into the water.

"What are you doing?" the bear asked.

"I am fishing," the fox replied. "Would you like to try?"

The bear loved fish, so he was very eager to try.

"This is what you must do," the crafty fox explained. "Put your lovely long tail in the hole. Soon a fish will grab it, and then you can pull the fish out. In the meantime, you must be very patient and stay perfectly still."

The bear was hungry and wanted to catch some fish, so he did exactly as the fox had told him.

The next morning, the fox went back to the lake and saw that the bear was lying on the ice. He was fast asleep and covered in snow. The hole had frozen over during the night and now the bear's tail was trapped in the ice.

The fox called out, "You've caught a fish! Quick! Pull out your tail!"

The bear woke up with a start and tugged his tail as hard as he could. All of a sudden, there was a loud CRACK! as the bear's frozen tail snapped off.

And that explains why bears now have very short tails and why they are definitely not friends with foxes!

Bedtime Adventure

Leah and Megan were not only twin sisters – they were best friends, and they played together all day long.

At bedtime, the twins couldn't wait to wake up and have more fun again in the morning.

One night, as Leah settled down on the top bunk bed, she made a wish upon a star.

"I wish we could play together in our sleep, too," she whispered.

That night, Leah was dreaming of playing with mermaids when, suddenly, she saw Megan flying around the room.

"Are you really flying?" Leah asked, rubbing her eyes.

"Yes," said Megan with a grin. "Come and play!"

Leah jumped out of bed and floated up to the ceiling. Megan took her hand and the window opened, as if by magic.

Together the twins flew out into the sky.

The sisters slid down some moonbeams and dived into the sea. They swam underwater with some fish, while mermaids with silvery tails darted along beside them.

"Let's be mermaids, too," said Leah.

Their legs started to sparkle until they turned into mermaid tails. Leah and Megan flicked and twisted their tails as they followed the mermaids to a big rock. Then they all pulled themselves onto the rock. They ran gem-encrusted combs through their hair, and sang beautiful songs that made dolphins dance in the water below.

Slowly, the stars faded and the sky grew brighter. The night was nearly over…and it was time for the sisters to go home.

Leah opened her eyes and looked down at Megan, who was grinning up at her from the bottom bunk bed.

"Was it all just a dream?" she asked in a whisper.

"Of course," said Megan. "But we both remember it, and I can't wait for our next bedtime adventure!"

The Penny Wise Monkey

Once upon a time, there lived a king who ruled over a rich and prosperous kingdom. But the king was never happy with what he had. He always wanted more.

One day, he set out with his men on yet another mission to take over yet another kingdom. They trekked through the forest all day. By the evening, they were exhausted and stopped to take some rest.

After supper, the soldiers fed their horses apples. In a nearby tree, a hungry monkey watched them. Some of the apples fell on the ground. The monkey jumped down from the tree, grabbed a handful of them, and scampered back up to the top.

As he sat enjoying the apples, one slipped from his hand and fell to the ground. Without thinking, the greedy monkey dropped all the other apples in his hands and ran down to look for the lost apple. He couldn't find it, and climbed back up the tree, empty-handed. His greed made him lose all that he had.

The king, who had been watching the monkey closely, realised that his own need to have more and more might also leave him with nothing one day.

"I will not be like this foolish monkey, who lost so much to gain so little!" he cried. "I will go back to my own kingdom and enjoy what I have."

The Monkeys and the Moon

A long, long time ago, a band of monkeys lived in a forest. In the middle of the forest there was a deep well.

One night, when the leader of the monkeys went to the well to get a drink, he saw the reflection of the moon in the water.

"Oh no!" he gasped. "The moon has fallen in the water. Our sky will have no moon. We must get it out!"

The other monkeys agreed. They formed a chain, each holding on to the tail of the one before them, while the monkey at the top of the chain held on to a branch to support them all.

The branch began to bend under the weight of all the monkeys. Suddenly... CRACK! The branch broke and the monkeys tumbled into the well. The water rippled as they all scrambled to get out of the well, and the reflection of the moon disappeared.

Up above the forest, the moon shone its silvery light on the silly, wet monkeys!

The Gnome

Once upon a time, there was a king who had a special apple tree in his palace garden. The fruit was delicious, but the tree was cursed. The king forbade anyone, including his own three daughters, to eat the apples: if they did, they would find themselves at the bottom of a deep well.

Of course, his daughters couldn't resist the sweet fruits, and they each ate an apple.

In a flash, the three girls disappeared deep underground. When they didn't return home that evening, the king was distraught. He put out a proclamation saying he would offer a huge reward for their safe return.

Three young huntsmen, who were also brothers, set out to look for the princesses. They had been travelling for a few days when they came across a cottage in the forest. There was no sign of anyone living there, and as the two elder brothers didn't like their youngest brother, Hans, they told him to stay at the cottage in case anyone came home. Then they went out to look for the princesses, hoping to get the reward for themselves.

The brothers hadn't been gone long when a strange little gnome appeared in front of Hans. He told the younger brother where the princesses were hidden and how to rescue them.

"The princesses are at the bottom of a deep well in the middle of this forest," explained the gnome. "But go alone because your brothers will betray you."

Hans did as he was told and he soon found the princesses. They were very happy to see him.

That evening, when Hans' brothers returned to the cottage, they were furious to see that Hans had found the princesses himself. So they told Hans to go home, then they took the princesses back to the palace, where they told the king that they had rescued the princesses. But the princesses wanted to thank Hans – their real rescuer – so they told their father the truth.

As punishment, the king banished the two elder brothers from his kingdom for good. Then he rewarded Hans with a huge pot of gold.

And, just to be safe, the king had the apple tree cut down!

Rebecca Rabbit's Birthday Wish

Rebecca Rabbit had just one wish for her birthday. She didn't want presents or even a party.

"Please, please, please," she whispered, "let me have the biggest carrot cake in the world!" But Rebecca was so busy wishing for the cake that she forgot to tell her friends that this was what she really wanted.

On the day of Rebecca's birthday, her friends surprised her with a big party. There were piles of presents and sparkling party hats. But she couldn't see a single cake. Rebecca couldn't help feeling a tiny bit disappointed. She didn't see her friends smiling and winking at each other.

First, Rosie Rabbit held out a very large box. When Rebecca opened it, she found a big cake inside. It was lovely, but it had only one layer.

"Thank you," said Rebecca with a smile.

It wasn't the enormous cake she had dreamed about, but it looked delicious. She knew that Rosie must have worked really hard to bake it.

Then Rex Rabbit held out his present. Rebecca opened it and found another cake, a little smaller than the first.

"I can put it on top of the other cake," she said, starting to feel really excited. Her birthday cake would have two tiers!

One by one, she opened her presents, and each one was a new cake. Hopping with excitement, Rebecca placed them one on top of the other, until the cake was towering above her.

"It really is the biggest carrot cake in the world!" she whispered.

Then, when her friends sang 'Happy Birthday', Rebecca climbed to the top of the cake and blew out her candles. But she didn't make a wish.

"I already have everything I want..." she said happily, "an enormous cake and the greatest friends in the world! Thank you, everyone."

87

The Lost Shark

Thalia the clownfish and her friends were always being chased by sharks. One day, Thalia saw a baby shark on its own. None of Thalia's friends would help him.

"We don't like sharks," they said.

Thalia felt sorry for the baby. He looked so sad.

Trembling, she whispered, "Are you all right?"

"I've lost my mummy," the baby shark cried.

Thalia had never seen a baby with so many sharp teeth. But she imagined how scared he must feel.

"Come on," she said. "I'll help you find her."

Before long, they found the mummy shark. She had been swimming around, looking for her little one.

"Oh, you've found him," she said to Thalia. Then she bared her teeth... and smiled. Then she added, "Thank you!"

Thalia and the baby shark made friends, and Thalia soon found out that the sharks had only been chasing the fish to play.

"Sharks aren't so bad after all!" Thalia said.

Granny's Garden

One day, when Megan visited her granny, no one answered the door. Feeling curious, Megan walked around the side of the house and into the garden. On the grass, she saw half a pumpkin, a spindle, a glass slipper and a mermaid comb. There was even a pot of gold with a rainbow bursting out of it.

"That's odd!" thought Megan. "I've not seen these here before."

Then, all of a sudden, Granny flew across the sky, holding a wand and wearing wings. Megan's mouth fell open.

"You're a fairy godmother!" Megan gasped.

"I'm the fairy godmother," said Granny. "I've just come back from visiting Cinderella, and now I have to dash out for tea with my fairy friends. Next time you visit, I'll tell you all about it. But for now, promise to keep my secret?"

"Of course!" gasped Megan.

Then Granny waved her wand and disappeared in a swirl of sparkles.

Megan couldn't wait for her next trip to Granny's house!

The Wild Swans

Once upon a time, in a distant land, there lived a king. He was blessed with eleven sons and one daughter, Elisa. Sadly, his wife had died. But the king was a loving father and the children were happy.

One day, however, everything changed. The king decided to marry again. His new wife was cruel, but the king was blind to her evil ways. She had Elisa sent away to live with a poor family in the forest, and the princes banished from the kingdom. She cast an enchantment on the boys, transforming them into wild swans. They flew away, wondering sadly if they would ever see their sister again.

The years passed. Elisa was never allowed to return home, and every day her heart ached to see her brothers again.

On her fifteenth birthday, she decided to go in search of the princes.

Elisa walked through the forest until she reached the shores of the ocean. As she gazed at the sun setting below the sea, eleven wild swans landed on the sand. Elisa gasped as the swans suddenly transformed into her brothers.

"Whenever the sun is up, we live as swans," the eldest brother explained. "Only at nightfall may we return to our human form. We live across the ocean now, far away. Come home with us."

So Elisa went to live with her swan brothers.

One night, she had a strange dream. A fairy told her that she must make a nettle shirt for each brother. Once they put it on, the spell would be broken and they would be men again. But Elisa was to stay silent until her work was finished, otherwise her brothers would die.

When Elisa awoke, she started on her task straightaway.
She didn't utter a word, even though the nettles stung her hands.
She worked hard all day. Just as she was about to return to her
brothers, a group of huntsmen, led by a king, appeared.

The king fell in love with Elisa at first sight.

"Come with me to my palace and be
my queen," he said.

As Elisa was sworn to silence,
she couldn't protest.

Holding the nettle shirts, she reluctantly left with the king.

"Your Majesty, you cannot marry this girl," the archbishop complained. "There is witchcraft at work here, mark my words!"

That night, Elisa tried to sneak out of the palace, but the archbishop caught her and brought her before the king.

"The girl is up to something, Your Majesty," cried the archbishop. "She is a witch!"

The king was heartbroken. Elisa dared not speak to defend herself, and so she was condemned to death.

At sunrise, still clutching the nettle shirts, Elisa was taken to her place of execution. Suddenly, eleven swans swooped down from the sky. Elisa threw the shirts over her swan brothers. They instantly changed into young men.

"Now I may speak," Elisa exclaimed. "I am no witch. All I ever wanted was to break an evil curse and free my brothers."

The king was shocked by this.

"My true love," he cried. "Can you ever forgive me?"

Elisa nodded. The spell had been broken. She had her brothers back, and she knew she would never be unhappy again.

Pink is for Princesses

Princess Ava didn't like pink, which was a problem, because every single thing that anybody ever gave her was pink. Her bedroom was pink. Her clothes were pink. Even her hairbrush was pink. And one day, she decided that enough was enough.

"No more pink!" said Princess Ava in her firmest voice.

"Don't be silly," said her father, the king. "Pink is the best colour for a princess."

"But I want to wear red and green and blue and purple!" Princess Ava pleaded.

The king shook his head.

"I won't allow it," he said stubbornly.

But Princess Ava was even more stubborn than her father. She put on her pink cloak, pulled her pink hood up so no one could recognize her and marched off to the market. There were lots of stalls selling clothes and shoes and blankets and trinkets and balls of string in every colour that she could imagine.

Princess Ava bought sky-blue and grass-green gowns. She picked out white and blue shoes. She chose golden blankets and deep-blue curtains.

"Who is that girl?" whispered the market sellers.

Back at the palace, Princess Ava collected up everything pink to be given away, and filled her room with every other colour of the rainbow.

When the king saw Princess Ava's room, his eyes nearly popped out of his head. But then he looked at his daughter's big smile, and he smiled too.

"You were right," he said. "I'm sorry. These bright colours are perfect for you, and I love to see you looking happy."

And from that day on, no one gave Princess Ava anything pink ever again!

Crocodile Teeth

Chloe Crocodile was getting ready for bedtime. "Will the Tooth Fairy come tonight?" she asked her mummy.

"Your tooth hasn't fallen out yet," her mummy replied, and she kissed Chloe goodnight.

As Chloe lay by the creek, she wobbled her tooth, but it wouldn't budge. Would it ever fall out? Suddenly, a tiny fairy fluttered out from behind a leaf and landed on Chloe's nose.

"I'm Kitty the Tooth Fairy," she said. "Can I help?"

Chloe's mouth fell open in surprise. Kitty reached in and gave the tooth an expert twist and – hey presto! It was out! Kitty put it into her pocket.

"This deserves a very special coin indeed," said Kitty. "Look under your pillow in the morning."

Then Kitty said goodbye and fluttered away as quickly as she had appeared.

The next day, Chloe found a crocodile coin under her pillow, with a little note that said: "Even crocodiles have visits from the Tooth Fairy." Chloe couldn't wait to show her mummy!

The Stone Soup

Samuel was on his way to visit a friend, but he was cold, tired and hungry. Up ahead, he saw a little cottage.

"Please could you spare me some food?" he asked the owner of the cottage.

"I don't have any," lied the old woman.

"Could I borrow your pot and cook some tasty soup?" Samuel asked.

"You may, if you share it with me," replied the old woman.

So Samuel filled the pot with water. Then he found two large stones outside. He cleaned them and put them in the pot.

"What kind of soup are you making?" asked the old woman in surprise.

"Stone soup," replied Samuel. "It's wonderful, but it would taste even better with some vegetables."

"I've got carrots and potatoes," the old woman said.

Samuel added the vegetables and stirred the soup.

Then he said, "With seasoning, it would be perfect!"

"I've got salt and pepper," replied the old woman.

Soon the soup was ready. "Hmm, delicious," said the old woman, not realising she was sharing her food after all!

Bird Bear

Isla was a little bear cub. She lived in the woods with her mummy and daddy, and her big sister. One day, she was playing with her sister when she saw some blue tits swooping out of their nest, high up in a tree. Isla stared at the birds as they glided and fluttered and flew. Then she gave a deep, long sigh.

"I want to fly like that," she said.

"Bears can't fly," said her sister.

"Then I don't want to be a bear any more," Isla said. "I want to be a blue tit and fly through the sky, and live in a nest in a tree."

Isla's sister just shook her head. She knew that bears couldn't turn into birds. But Isla couldn't stop thinking about it. She climbed up the tree and watched the birds all afternoon. Her sister got fed up and wandered off, but Isla didn't care.

"Birds have wings," she said to herself. "If I make myself some wings, maybe I'll be able to fly too."

She pulled two leafy branches off the tree and climbed down. Holding one in each hand, Isla started to run, flapping the branches up and down as fast as she could. But she didn't raise a single toe off the ground. Feeling gloomy, she walked back towards home, trailing the branches behind her.

On the way, Isla spotted a finch pecking the ground. As she watched, the finch pulled a worm out of the ground and swallowed it whole. Then it flew away.

"Hmm," said Isla. "Perhaps I need to learn to be a bird in other ways before I can fly."

She dropped the branches and knelt down on the ground. After a long wait, she saw a worm poking through the soil. With a single gulp, she swallowed it down. It tasted horrible!

"Yuck!" she growled. "Yuck! Yuck! Yuck! Why do birds eat worms? Someone should tell them about honey!"

Just then, a blackbird nearby started to sing.

"That's it!" Isla exclaimed. "I will learn to sing as sweetly as a bird!"

She opened her mouth as wide as it would go, and began to sing in her highest voice.

"ARRRGHHH! EEEEEE! OOOOOOH!" All the animals nearby dived for cover. The birds shot up out of the trees in fright. A rabbit poked her head out of a hole in the ground and glared at Isla.

"Stop making that awful noise!" she snapped. "My babies are asleep!"

"I'm sorry," said Isla. "I was trying to sing like a bird."

"Well, it didn't work," said the rabbit in a cross voice. "If I were you, I'd stop trying to be something you're not."

Suddenly, Isla felt very tired. She was about to sit down for a rest when she saw her mummy gathering honeycombs for supper. She clambered onto her mummy's back and held on tight.

"What a tired bear," said her mummy. "Have you had a busy day?"

"Very busy," said Isla, yawning. "Mummy, why can't I be a bird and fly around?"

"Because you're a bear cub, and that's what you do best," said her mummy. "Now, shall I carry you home and tell you all about the trees we're going to climb tomorrow? I know where to find all the biggest honeycombs."

Isla nodded and snuggled into her mummy's cosy fur.

Night started to fall, and the moon came out. Isla yawned again. She still thought that being able to fly like a bird would be wonderful. But being able to climb trees and eat honeycombs with her mummy was even better!

Cleo and the Unicorn

Cleo dreamed of meeting a unicorn.

"They don't exist," said Cleo's mum.

"You're being silly," said her brother.

Even her dad smiled and patted her on the head.

One day, Cleo was playing in the garden when she heard a snorting noise behind the shed. She went to find out what it was and saw a small, muddy animal.

"Hello," said Cleo in a gentle voice. "What are you?" She carefully picked up the creature. "You're a tiny pony!" she exclaimed. "Let me clean you up, little one."

Cleo bathed the pony in her paddling pool. Underneath all the dirt, the pony was as white as snow. Cleo wrapped it in her best fleecy blanket and read it a story until it fell asleep. Then she looked up and gasped in surprise. A shining white unicorn was standing beside the shed!

"I've always wanted to see a unicorn," whispered Cleo.

"You already have," said the unicorn with a smile. "You are cuddling my baby. I have been searching for him all day."

"But he doesn't have a horn," said Cleo.

"Unicorn horns don't grow until we're older," said the unicorn. "Thank you for taking care of him."

Cleo unfolded the blanket and the little unicorn woke up. He trotted happily to his mummy.

"Will I ever see him again?" Cleo asked.

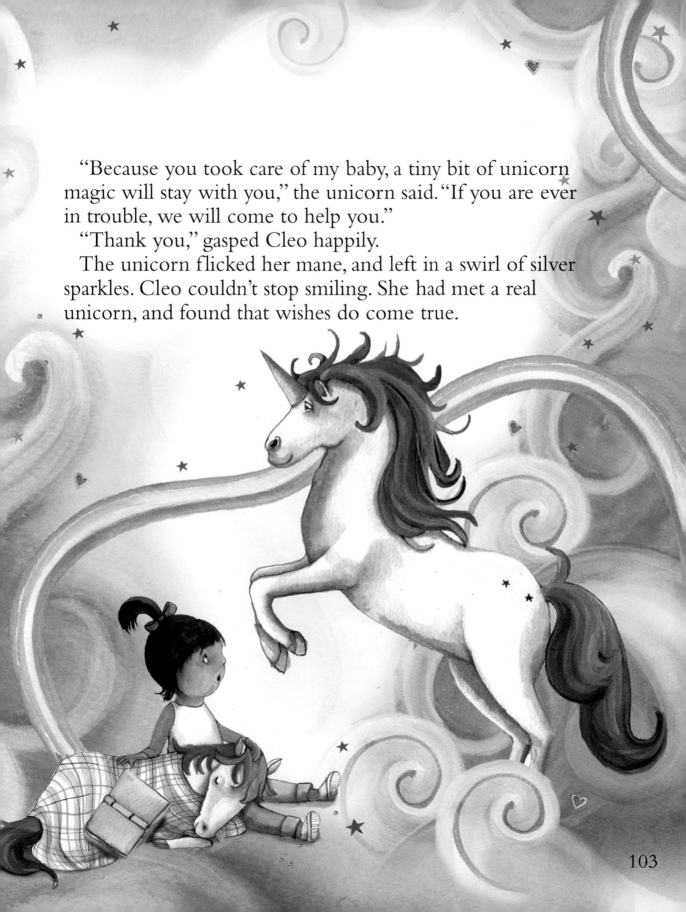

"Because you took care of my baby, a tiny bit of unicorn magic will stay with you," the unicorn said. "If you are ever in trouble, we will come to help you."

"Thank you," gasped Cleo happily.

The unicorn flicked her mane, and left in a swirl of silver sparkles. Cleo couldn't stop smiling. She had met a real unicorn, and found that wishes do come true.

The Enormous Pancake

Once upon a time, there was a woman who had seven little boys. They were always hungry.

"If you are very good," said their mother, "I will make you the biggest pancake you have ever seen!"

So she cracked the eggs, measured the milk, weighed the flour and mixed it all together. Then she poured the mixture into a hot pan. The pancake was going to be enormous!

When it was time to flip it over, the hungry little boys cried out, "Toss it in the air, Mother, please!"

So their mother tossed the pancake high into the air.

But the pancake didn't want to be eaten, so with a flip and a flop it landed on the floor and rolled out of the door.

"Stop!" cried the hungry little boys. "We want to eat you!"

But the pancake didn't want to be eaten. So it rolled down the road, with the boys and their mother chasing after it.

Soon, the pancake passed a cat.

"Stop!" miaowed the cat, licking her lips. "You would taste yummy washed down with a bowl of milk. Let me eat you."

But the pancake just rolled faster. "Seven little boys and their mother couldn't catch me, and you won't either!" it shouted. So the cat chased after it.

Next, the pancake passed a duck pond.

"Stop!" quacked the duck. "I prefer pancakes to stale bread, so I'm going to eat you up!"

But the pancake rolled even faster. "Seven little boys, their mother and a cat couldn't catch me, and you won't either!" So the duck chased after it.

Then, the pancake passed a cow in a field.

"Stop!" mooed the cow. "I'll eat you instead of this grass!"

But the pancake rolled even faster still. "Seven little boys, their mother, a cat and a duck couldn't catch me, and you won't either!" So the cow chased after it.

Soon, the pancake met a pig by a river.

"Can you help me cross the river?" asked the pancake.

"Of course!" snorted the pig. "Sit on my nose and I'll carry you across." So the pancake jumped onto his nose.

In a flash, the pig flipped the pancake into the air and gobbled it up in one enormous GULP! "Yum!" said the pig.

Just then, the seven little boys, their mother, the cat, the duck and the cow arrived.

"Have you seen an enormous pancake?" they asked.

"Yes," snorted the pig happily, "and it was delicious!"

Best Friends' Christmas

Sarah and Rosina were best friends, and when they wrote their Christmas lists, they both asked for exactly the same thing: "A baby doll to play with, and one for my best friend too."

Not far away, in the toy factory, the toymakers were working hard to get ready for Christmas. They made piles of teddies and board games and baby dolls, and loaded them into sacks for Father Christmas to deliver. One morning, they got a surprise.

"Look at this!" said one of the toymakers, pointing at the dolls. "These two have made friends!"

Two baby dolls called Janey and Lucy were holding hands. The toymakers smiled, then pulled their hands away from each other and put them into different sacks. They didn't notice how sad the dolls looked.

On Christmas morning, Rosina unwrapped a big box and found Janey inside.

"I love her," said Rosina, cuddling Janey. "But she looks a bit sad."

She ran to Sarah's house at the end of the lane, and Sarah came running out to meet her. She was holding a baby doll that looked a bit sad too.

"This is Lucy," Sarah said.

Janey and Lucy were delighted to see each other again and their sad expressions changed. Rosina suddenly realised that the little dolls looked happy and were gazing at each other with sparkly eyes.

"I get the feeling that these two are going to be best friends, just like us," she said to Sarah.

"Perhaps they already are," said Sarah wisely.

Daisy and the Genie

Daisy bought an old tin lamp at a jumble sale.
"It just needs a quick polish and it will look as good as new again," she decided.

But when Daisy rubbed the lamp with a cloth, there was a loud bang and a puff of smoke. A small boy appeared with his arms folded across his chest.

"I am a genie!" he said. "I grant you three wishes!"

"Wow!" said Daisy. "How long have you been in the lamp?"

"I've been trapped for ages," the little genie admitted. "I'm training to be a genie. I was waiting for someone to rub the lamp and say their wishes, so I could return to Genie School."

"Can you really give me three wishes?" Daisy asked.

The genie nodded. "They might go wrong," he warned her. "I'm still learning. That's why I need to go back home."

"I wish for a new swing," Daisy began.

The genie snapped his fingers and a shiny new spring appeared in Daisy's hand.

"Oops!" said the genie. "That wasn't supposed to happen."

"Let's try something else," said Daisy with a laugh. "I wish for a house made of chocolate!"

Once again, the genie snapped his fingers and a large chocolate mouse appeared in Daisy's other hand.

"Oh dear," said the genie, sadly. "I'm not doing very well."
Daisy felt sorry for the little genie. She tried again.

"I wish for... a pet dog," she said finally.

The genie snapped his fingers and a frog appeared in Daisy's pocket. Daisy laughed, then noticed the genie was fading away.

"Where are you going?" she cried.

"I'm going back to Genie School," said the genie. "When a human makes three wishes, I can return. Thank you, Daisy!"

The genie and the lamp disappeared in a puff of smoke. Daisy looked at the spring, the chocolate mouse and the frog, and she smiled.

"You're welcome," she whispered.

Princess Elodie's Wish Hunt

Princess Elodie lived in Cloudland, and every day she chose which one of her beautiful cloud ponies she wanted to ride. Then she galloped around her kingdom to collect the wishes of children who had wished upon a star.

One morning, she found it very hard to decide which pony to ride. Should she choose Locket with her golden mane, or Emerald with her sparkling green eyes? The cloud ponies were all so beautiful. Then she heard a soft whinny and turned around. Behind her was a white pony with a curly mane that was as soft as the clouds.

"Hello, Cobweb," said Princess Elodie. "Would you like to go for a ride this morning?"

Cobweb whinnied again, so Princess Elodie fetched a saddle of blue satin.

"Let's go wish-hunting!" she said.

With Princess Elodie on his back, Cobweb galloped over the fluffy cloud hills and through the soft cloud meadows. Wishes were easy to spot because they looked like flowers, and the cloud bunnies loved to chase them.

Princess Elodie scooped up the wishes and put them in her pocket.

Just then, she spotted something half hidden among the cloud blossoms. After telling Cobweb to wait, she slipped down and brushed the blossoms aside. A little brown teddy was lying there, looking very sad.

"Poor lost teddy," said Princess Elodie, cuddling him tightly. "I'll look after you."

Cobweb carried Princess Elodie and the teddy back to the Cloud Palace. After Princess Elodie had removed the blue satin saddle and given Cobweb some food, she took the teddy into the palace. First she mended a tear along his arm and then she washed him and sat him beside the roaring fire to dry.

"Now," she said. "What shall I do with you?"

She emptied her pockets and the wishes spilled out over the palace floor. There were wishes for dolls, sunny days, fairgrounds and lots more, but Princess Elodie was looking for a very special wish. It took a long time to sort through and grant all the wishes, but at last she found what she was looking for. A lonely little boy had wished for a teddy bear friend.

Smiling, Princess Elodie went to fetch Cobweb. By the time she had brushed him down and saddled him, the teddy was dry. Princess Elodie tucked him under her arm, climbed onto Cobweb and held up the little boy's wish.

"Take us to the child who made this wish, please," she said.

Cobweb neighed and walked to the edge of Cloudland. A puffy cloud started to change shape, forming a set of steps that wound down through the night sky. Cobweb trotted down the cloud steps, while Elodie waved to the stars that twinkled all around them. The steps led them all the way to the little boy's bedroom window.

"Shhh," said Princess Elodie. She slipped off Cobweb's back onto the windowsill. Then she opened the window and stepped inside. The little boy was fast asleep in his bed, so Princess Elodie tucked the teddy into bed beside him. In his sleep, the boy smiled and put his arm around the teddy.

"Time to go," said Princess Elodie. She climbed out of the window and back onto Cobweb. Then he carried her up to Cloudland, where her swinging bed was hanging from the moon.

Yawning, Princess Elodie took Cobweb's saddle off and gave him a blanket and some food. Then she climbed onto her swing and drifted off to sleep, dreaming of the teddy and his happy new home.

Little Rabbit's Big Adventure!

Little Rabbit sat still in the tall grass. He glanced all around, but nothing looked familiar. Mummy Rabbit had told him not to go too far from the burrow. But, being a curious little bunny, he'd forgotten her words as soon as he'd seen the little buzzing bee fly by and had decided to follow it. Now he didn't know where he was.

"Oh no! I'm lost," cried Little Rabbit. "How will I get home?"

He looked around again. A beautiful pink butterfly was fluttering around some flowers nearby.

"Hello, Mrs Butterfly," called Little Rabbit. "I'm lost. Do you know where my burrow is?"

"Sorry, I don't," said the butterfly. "Try asking the sheep in that field."

"That's a good idea," replied Little Rabbit. He hopped off through the flowers and squeezed under a fence.

"Hello, Mrs Sheep," said Little Rabbit, "do you know where my burrow is?"

"No, I'm sorry, my dear," baaed the sheep.

Tears started to slide down Little Rabbit's face. "I miss my mummy, and I want to go home!"

"Don't cry," a squirrel called out from a tree at the edge of the field. "I know where your burrow is. Follow me."

"Oh, thank you, Mr Squirrel!" said Little Rabbit.

Little Rabbit followed the squirrel into the woods. After a little while the squirrel stopped.

"Here we are!" he said.

And there was Mummy Rabbit, standing by a small dark hole at the base of a big tree.

"Little Rabbit!" cried Mummy Rabbit, scooping him into her arms. "Where have you been? I've been so worried."

Little Rabbit told Mummy Rabbit all about his big adventure.

"What a brave bunny you are!" said Mummy.

Little Rabbit smiled and snuggled closer to his mummy. "But it's good to be back home."

115

The Loudest ROAR!

Leo the little lion cub wanted to be just like Daddy when he grew up.

"I'm going to have the loudest ROAR ever!" he said.

Daddy Lion grinned and patted Leo gently on the head with his large paw.

"Yes, one day you will," he said. "But while you are still little, why don't we go and play?"

"Teach me to roar like you first, Daddy, please!" pleaded Leo. He opened his little mouth but...

"GRRRRR!"

Leo could only make a tiny growling sound. The little lion cub stomped his paws on the ground in frustration.

"It needs to be louder, Daddy!" he cried.

Daddy lion smiled. "Don't worry, Leo, it will get louder with practice." Then he opened his mouth wide...

"RRRRRRROAR!"

The roar was so loud that the ground trembled under Leo's paws!

"GRRRRR!" Leo tried again.

"Sit up straight and tip your head back," advised Daddy. "And then open your mouth as wide as it will go..."

116

Leo watched Daddy Lion closely. He sat up straight, tipped his head back and opened his mouth as wide as it would go…

"RRRRRROAR!"

Leo could feel the ground trembling under his paws.

"That's my boy!" laughed Daddy. "You've got it!"

Leo was so happy with his new roar that he practised it all afternoon. Soon he was exhausted.

"That's enough for today," said Daddy as he settled Leo down for bed. "You don't want to lose your voice."

But Leo didn't hear him. He was already fast asleep, dreaming about his wonderful new loud roar!

Darcie's Treasure

Darcie's uncle was a treasure hunter. He used a special metal detector to search for riches.

One day, Darcie lost her necklace in the garden. So she asked her uncle if he could help her find it.

"Once, I discovered old coins and a medieval queen's jewellery in your garden," he told Darcie. "Legend says that she left a priceless golden goblet here too, but it's probably just a story."

Then Darcie's uncle showed her how to use the metal detector. When they reached the end of the garden, it beeped. Darcie and her uncle started to dig. They found a dirty old cup. When Darcie washed it, she saw that it was gold with red rubies around the side.

"The queen's goblet!" gasped her uncle.

Then the metal detector beeped again. This time they found Darcie's necklace. "You're going to be the best treasure hunter ever, Darcie!" said her uncle, with a grin.

Magic Museum

Zara loved the costume museum. She was fascinated by the clothes people wore hundreds of years ago, and the things they used in their homes. Best of all, she loved imagining that she lived in the old days too.

One day, during a visit, the guide asked Zara if she'd like to try something on. Feeling excited, Zara dressed up in a kitchen maid's uniform. Suddenly, the room around her disappeared and she found herself in a kitchen full of busy maids and butlers.

"Hurry up!" shouted the cook. "Don't dawdle!"

At first, Zara helped the cook prepare the food. But soon she was washing dishes and scrubbing floors. It was hard work! As Zara bent down, her cap fell off. And in a twinkling, the servants and the kitchen vanished. Zara was back in the museum.

"Will you come back tomorrow?" asked the guide.

"Yes, please. But I think a princess dress might suit me better!" said Zara, thinking about the kitchen from long ago.

Rapunzel

Once upon a time, a poor young couple lived in a cottage next door to an old witch. The witch grew many vegetables in her garden, but she kept them all for herself.

One day, the couple had only a few potatoes left to eat.

"Surely it wouldn't matter if we took just a few vegetables," said the wife, gazing longingly over the wall.

So her husband quickly climbed into the garden and started to fill his basket. Suddenly he heard an angry voice.

"How dare you steal my vegetables?"

"Please don't hurt me," begged the young man. "My wife is going to have a baby soon, and she is hungry!"

"You may keep the vegetables," she croaked. "But you must give me the baby when it is born."

Terrified, the man had to agree.

Months later, his wife gave birth to a little girl. And although the parents begged and cried, the cruel witch took the baby. She called her Rapunzel.

Years passed and Rapunzel grew up to be kind and beautiful. The witch was so afraid of losing her that she built a tall tower with no door and only one window. She planted thorn bushes all around it, then she locked Rapunzel in the tower.

Each day, Rapunzel brushed and combed her long golden locks. And each day, the witch came to visit her, standing at the foot of the tower and calling out, "Rapunzel, Rapunzel, let down your hair."

Rapunzel hung her hair out of the window and the witch climbed up it to sit and talk with her. But Rapunzel was very lonely. She sat at her window and sang sadly.

One day, a prince rode by and heard the beautiful singing coming from the witch's garden. As he hid behind the wall, he saw the old witch call out, "Rapunzel, Rapunzel, let down your hair."

The prince saw a cascade of golden hair fall from the tower, and he watched the witch climb up it.

When the witch returned to her house, he crept to the tower. "Rapunzel, Rapunzel, let down your hair," he called softly.

Rapunzel let down her locks and the prince climbed up.

Rapunzel was very surprised to see the prince, and delighted when he said he wanted to be her friend. From then on, the prince came to visit her every day.

Months passed and Rapunzel and the prince fell in love.

"How can we be together?" Rapunzel cried. "The witch will never let me go."

So the prince brought some silk which Rapunzel knotted together to make a ladder so that she could escape from the tower.

One day, without thinking, Rapunzel remarked to the witch, "It's much harder to pull you up than the prince!"

The witch was furious! "What prince?" she shouted.

She grabbed Rapunzel's long hair and cut it off. Then she used her magic to send Rapunzel far into the forest.

That evening, when the prince came to see Rapunzel, the witch held the golden hair out of the window and he climbed up into the tower, coming face to face with the old witch.

"You will never see Rapunzel again!" she screamed, and pushed the prince out of the window. He fell into the thorn bushes below. The sharp spikes scratched his eyes and blinded him. Weeping, he stumbled away.

After months of wandering, blind and lost, the prince heard beautiful, sad singing floating through the woods. He recognised Rapunzel's voice and called out to her.

"At last I have found you!" she cried. As her tears fell into the prince's eyes, his wounds healed, and he could see again.

Rapunzel had never been so happy. She and the prince were soon married, and they lived happily ever after, far away from the old witch and her empty tower.

The Clever Monkey

One day, Tiger was prowling through the jungle, looking for his lunch. He was just about to pounce on an unsuspecting deer, when his legs became trapped in a tangle of vines.

Poor Tiger was trying to think of a way to escape the trap, when he saw the deer he'd been hoping to eat for his lunch.

"Please help me, Deer!" he cried loudly. "Untangle the vines to set me free!"

Trembling, Deer shook her head.

"You'll eat me if I set you free."

"I promise I won't," said Tiger. "We can be friends."

Deer thought it would be better to have Tiger as a friend, rather than an enemy, so she untangled the vines.

But as soon as Tiger was free, he pounced on Deer.

"You promised not to eat me!" pleaded Deer.

"But I'm hungry!" roared Tiger.

Deer started to sob.

"What's going on?" asked Monkey, who was passing nearby. He'd heard Deer crying.

"Monkey," sniffed Deer, "do you think it is right for Tiger to eat me when I have just saved his life?"

"You did not save my life!" roared Tiger.

"Well, tigers do usually like to eat deer," replied Monkey. "Tiger, why don't you show me where you were, and then I can see if Deer really saved your life."

Grumbling to himself, Tiger let Deer tie the vines around his legs to show Monkey where he had been trapped.

Quick as a flash, Monkey jumped onto Deer's back.

"Come on, Deer," he chuckled. "Let's go!"
"Thanks, Monkey," said Deer. "Now you've saved my life!"
Tiger roared loudly as he found himself trapped once more.

The Golden Goose

There was once a man who had three sons. Two of them were clever, but everyone thought the youngest, called Peter, was silly.

One day, the father sent the eldest son, Luke, into the forest to chop down a tree. He was just about to start work when a little old man appeared.

"Please can I have some food?" the old man asked.

"If I give some to you, there won't be much for me," Luke replied. Then he began to chop down the tree.

As if by magic, the eldest son's axe slipped and he cut his arm, so he had to go home.

As the wood still needed chopping, the father sent the middle son, Paul, into the forest. Once again, the little old man appeared.

"Please can I have some food?" asked the old man.

But the middle son refused. "I won't have much left if I give some to you," he replied.

Suddenly, Paul's axe slipped and he cut his leg. So he had to go home, too.

"Father, let me chop down the tree," said Peter.

His father laughed. "What makes you think you can do it if your brothers can't?"

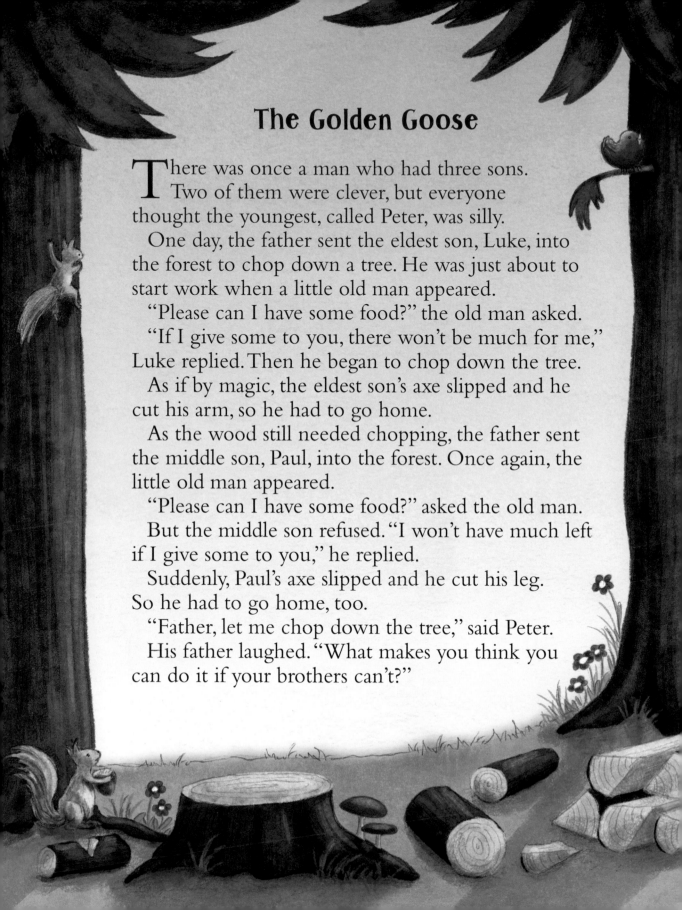

But Peter begged his father until he gave in.

Peter set off to the forest. It wasn't long before he met the little old man.

"Please can I have some food?" asked the old man.

"There's not much," Peter said. "But you are welcome to share it with me."

"You're a kind boy," said the old man, as they sat down to eat. "Let me give you something in return."

The old man told Peter to cut down the tree and see what was inside its roots.

Peter did as the old man said. Inside the roots was a goose with golden feathers. Puzzled, Peter looked around for the old man, but he had mysteriously disappeared.

By now it was getting late, so Peter picked up the goose and went to find an inn for the night.

The innkeeper had three daughters and they were fascinated by the goose's golden feathers. One by one, they reached out to pluck a golden feather, but the moment they touched the bird, they stuck to the goose and couldn't let go!

In the morning, the girls were still stuck to the goose. So Peter set out for home, with the three girls trailing behind him.

When other people saw the strange procession, they tried to pull the girls free, only to become stuck too!

Peter's journey took him through a city ruled by a king. The king's daughter was so sad and the king couldn't make her happy. In desperation, he offered her hand in marriage to anyone who could make her laugh.

As soon as the princess saw Peter's ridiculous procession, she began to laugh as if she would never stop.

The king was thrilled. "You may marry my daughter!" he told Peter.

So Peter and the princess soon married. They lived a happy life, full of laughter, and no one made fun of Peter any more.

The Magic Sky

One icy Arctic night, Lila and Poko the polar bear cubs were getting ready for bed. It was freezing outside, but it was cosy and warm inside their den. The two cubs snuggled down beside their mother and closed their eyes. They were almost asleep, when they heard a noise outside.

"Psst! Lila! Poko!" said a voice. It was their friend Tiki the Arctic hare.

"Come outside! Quickly!" whispered Tiki. "There is something I want to show you. Something very peculiar is happening. I think there must be magic in the air."

"What's going on?" yawned Mother Bear sleepily.

"Something magical is happening," replied Tiki. "I can't describe it. You must come and see for yourself."

"Ah," smiled Mother Bear. "I think I know what it is. Let's all go and take a look together."

The three sleepy polar bears crawled out of their den and padded across the icy snow. Lila and Poko looked around in surprise. Everything looked so different. The icy landscape was bathed in a strange glow.

"Look up," whispered Tiki.

The polar bear cubs looked up and gasped in amazement. Something very strange was happening in the sky above. It was full of dancing lights, swirling and twirling around above their heads. They all stared in wonder, unable to speak at first.

"It's beautiful!" gasped Poko eventually.

"What's happening?" asked Lila.

"It's the Northern Lights!" said Mother Bear.

"Is it magic?" asked Poko excitedly. "We love magic."

Mother Bear thought for a while and then smiled.

"Yes," she agreed. "It's the magic of nature!"

Small World

Elizabeth and Jamie were best friends, and they loved playing together in the woods behind their homes.

One day, when they were in Jamie's front garden, Jamie saw a little grasshopper on the pavement outside. He picked him up with gentle hands.

"You might get trodden on if you stay there," Jamie told him. "We'll help you. We know how it feels to be small."

So Jamie and Elizabeth put the little grasshopper on some grass at the side of the pavement.

"Thank you," said the grasshopper. "You are very kind."

Jamie couldn't believe his ears. His mouth fell open in amazement.

"You can talk!" he exclaimed.

"All animals can talk," said the grasshopper. "We just don't choose to talk to humans very often. Would you like to come to the woods with me? I will take you to the Land of Animals. No human has ever visited it before!"

"We'd love to," said Elizabeth.

The grasshopper jumped ahead of them and they ran down the path behind him, giggling as they chased the little green creature into the woods.

They ran and jumped over bracken and logs, until the grasshopper stopped beside a small green leaf. It had a hole in the middle of it.

The grasshopper tapped the leaf with one of his wings, and the leaf grew until the hole was the size of a door. The grasshopper turned and smiled at them.

"Welcome to my home!" he said.

He hopped through the hole, and the children followed him.

Everything was different through the hole. The sky was bluer. The grass was greener. Even the sun shone a little more brightly. Best of all, everywhere the children looked, they saw animals. Everyone was playing happily. Butterflies danced together, making beautiful patterns and shapes with their wings. Bunnies hopped around them, and birds landed on their shoulders, singing their merriest songs.

"Look at the ladybirds!" cried Elizabeth. They were looping the loop and twisting and diving through the air.

Tiny brown bunny rabbits hopped around the trees, playing catch and hide-and-seek. When they saw the children, they stopped and waved their paws.

"Come and play with us!" they called.

Elizabeth and Jamie could hardly wait! They followed the rabbits as they bounded around the trees, and ran deeper into the Land of Animals.

The children hid among flowering bushes, and the rabbits looked for them, thumping their big feet in delight when they won.

Elizabeth and Jamie made friends with speckled deer, and climbed trees with the squirrels to look for nuts. Finally, the light faded, and owls peered out from trees with sleepy eyes.

"Time to go home," they hooted. "The grasshopper will be waiting for you."

Elizabeth and Jamie hurried back to the leaf with the big hole in it. The grasshopper was there, right beside the magical leaf.

"Did you have a good time?" he asked.

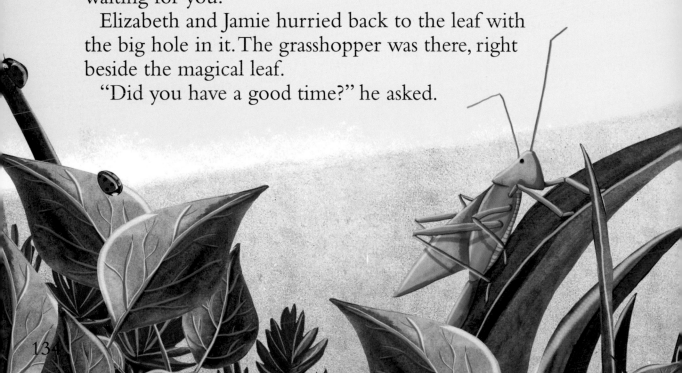

"It's been the most amazing day ever," said Elizabeth. "We've loved every moment."

"And we've loved having you visit the Land of Animals," the grasshopper replied. "You are very special. Not many humans remember how it feels to be small."

"We will never forget," said Jamie as they stepped back through the magical leaf door. "We promise!"

Unicorn Magic

Once upon a time, there were two little unicorns called Lottie and Lulu, and they lived with their mother in a cave on top of a mountain.

Unicorns are magical creatures and their twisty horns are full of spells and enchantments. But little unicorns have to learn how to use their magic…and they don't always get it right!

One day, Lottie and Lulu's mother went to visit some friends. As soon as she had trotted out of sight, Lottie and Lulu shared a big smile.

"Let's give her a surprise," said Lottie. "Let's magically tidy up the cave."

Lottie said the first spell, and purple sparkles flew out of her twisty horn and hit a messy heap of hay in the corner. But instead of tidying it up, the spell turned the hay purple.

"Let me try," said Lulu. As she said her spell, green sparkles zipped out of her twisty horn and hit a bowl of apples. They turned into beetles and scuttled off.

"Let's do the dusting," said Lottie. She tried to make the dust vanish, but it turned into a cloud of glitter instead.

"Oh no! What a mess," gasped Lulu.

Things got worse and worse. Every spell that Lottie and Lulu tried went wrong. They made their beds with honey instead of heather. They covered the ceiling with blue cornflowers. They turned the ribbons that their mother decorated her mane with into butterflies.

And that was when their mother came back.

"Oh dear," she said, looking around at the chaos.

"We're sorry," said Lulu. "We were trying to help, but every spell went wrong."

Their mother nuzzled them both.

"It's all right," she said. "It is a bit messy, but I don't think I have ever seen the cave looking so pretty and colourful!"

137

Princess Bea's Wish

Princess Bea didn't like getting messy. She would rather play in her bedroom, where everything was neat and tidy, than go outside and get muddy.

Then, on Bea's birthday, her fairy godmother gave her three magic wishes.

"Thank you!" Princess Bea said. "My first two wishes are a doll's house and a toy puppy."

Bea's fairy godmother waved her wand and, with a tinkle of silver bells, the new toys magically appeared.

Bea started playing with them, but they weren't as much fun as she had hoped.

"I'm bored of playing indoors," she thought.

So she went for a ride in her carriage. Soon she saw the village children sitting by the stream, looking sad. Bea stopped the carriage and got out.

"What's wrong?" she asked them.

"The rope swing over the stream has broken," said one of the children. "We've got nothing to play on."

Bea thought hard. She had lots of toys. She didn't really need her third wish.

"I wish for the rope swing to be repaired," she whispered.

Suddenly, there was a magical flash and lots of rope swings appeared over the river. The children squealed in delight.

"Come and play with us!" they called to Bea.

Bea thought it might be fun, so she did.

Later, when the princess went home, her dress was torn, her knees were muddy and her hair was full of brambles.

She had even lost one of her shoes!

"What a messy princess!" said her fairy godmother, smiling. "Did you have a good time?"

"Yes, thank you," said Bea. "Today was the best birthday ever! I had so much fun with my new friends, I forgot all about getting messy."

Little Dragon Goes to School

Little Dragon bounced out of bed. Today was his very first day of school! He was a little bit excited. First, he had a big bowl of breakfast, then he washed, sploshed and brushed his teeth.

School was big, and Little Dragon felt very little. Then he saw his best friends, Prince Pip and Princess Pippa.

"Hello, it's me!" said Little Dragon.

"Get to the back of the line!" said Little Baron Boris.

When the bell rang, they all went inside. There was a row of coat pegs with little pictures over them. Little Dragon liked the piggy peg.

"That's my peg!" said Little Baron Boris. "Get your own!"

So Little Dragon hung his bag on the spider peg instead.

They all sat in a circle and the nice teacher, Miss Plum, called out their names.

"Little Dragon?" she said.

"Hello, it's me!" said Little Dragon. Everyone giggled.

Miss Plum showed them how to write their names. Little Dragon tried...and tried...but...it was tricky!

Soon it was time for lunch.

"I've forgotten my lunch!" said Little Dragon.

"You can share our sandwiches – we've got lots!" said Pip and Pippa.

"You can have my horrible pickle," said Little Baron Boris.

After lunch they did painting. Prince Pip painted a tiger. Princess Pippa painted a flower. Little Dragon painted Boris's bottom and a pink pig!

When everybody was clean again they all sat down. Then Miss Plum read them a funny story about a big bad troll and a clever little goat. Little Dragon felt happy and sleepy.

Soon it was time to go home. Little Dragon found his spider peg and got his bag. He said goodbye to Miss Plum and went outside. Then he started to cry.

"I wish I could come to school again tomorrow," he sniffled.

"You can!" said Pippa, "Every day except for holidays!"

"Yippee!" shouted Little Dragon. "I like school!"

The Perfect Pet

Emily was visiting her friend Ethan's farm to choose a puppy. Most of the puppies bounded around the barn, barking and jumping on each other. But one puppy gently pressed against Emily's legs and licked her knees.

"I like this one," said Emily, looking at the puppy's cute brown fur.

"Are you sure?" asked Ethan. "Rusty doesn't chase sticks and run around like the other puppies."

Rusty's ears drooped and he pressed closer to Emily. It was true he wasn't like the others. But Emily looked down at his sad eyes and smiled at him.

"Look, he's so gentle and kind," said Emily, tickling Rusty's ears. "He's the perfect pet for me!"

Rusty's heart leaped with happiness and he wagged his little tail. And Emily knew that she had found the most perfect pet in the whole, wide world.

The Secret Cat Circus

Every morning, when they went to work, Jessie's owners left her dozing in the sunniest corner of the garden. They thought she was a very sleepy cat, but Jessie had a secret. As soon as they had gone, Jessie pulled on a sparkly costume and went to work too…at the cat circus hidden at the bottom of their garden!

"Roll up!" the tabby circus master shouted to the gathering crowd. "Come and see the best tightrope-walking cat in the whole wide world!"

The crowd gasped as Jessie walked the tightrope, balancing a fish on her nose and juggling balls of string.

By five o'clock the circus show was over and Jessie pulled off her costume, settling down to doze in the sun for when her owners came home.

"That cat could sleep all day!" Jessie's owners cried each evening.

Little did they know of her performing talent – or where the sparkles in her fur came from!

Puss in Boots

There was once an old miller who had three sons. When the miller died, he left the mill to his oldest son. The middle son was given the donkeys. The youngest son, a kind man who had always put his father and brothers before himself, was left nothing but his father's cat.

"What will become of me?" sighed the miller's young son, looking at his cat.

"Buy me a fine pair of boots and I will help you make your fortune, just as your father had wished," replied the cat.

A talking cat! The miller's son could not believe his ears.

He bought the cat a fine pair of boots and the two of them set off to seek their fortune.

After a while, they came to a grand palace.

"I wish I could live so grandly," sighed the miller's son.

Later, the cat went hunting and caught a rabbit. He put it in a sack and took it to the king.

"A gift from my master, the Marquis of Carabas," said the cat, pretending the miller's son was a grand nobleman.

"Now the king will want to know all about you," laughed the cat, when he told his master what he had done.

The cat delivered gifts all that week, and the king became very curious. So much so, he decided his daughter should meet this mysterious Marquis of Carabas.

The clever cat rushed back to his master, telling him to take off all his clothes and stand in the river by the side of the road.

The puzzled miller's son did as he was told and the cat quickly hid his master's tattered clothes behind a rock.

When the cat heard the king's carriage coming, he jumped out into the road.

"Your Majesty," cried the cat, "my master's clothes were stolen while he was bathing in the river."

The king gave the miller's son a suit of fine clothes to wear and invited him into the carriage.

The miller's son looked very handsome in his new suit and the king's daughter fell in love with him at once.

Meanwhile, the cat quickly ran on ahead. Every time he met people working in the fields, he told them, "If the king stops to ask who owns this land, you must tell him it belongs to the Marquis of Carabas."

Beyond the fields, the cat reached a grand castle belonging to a fierce ogre. The cat bravely knocked on the door and called out, "I have heard that you are a very clever ogre and I would like to see what tricks you can do."

The ogre, who liked to show off his tricks, immediately changed himself into a snarling lion.

"Very clever," said the cat, "but a lion is large, and I think it would be more impressive to change into a tiny mouse."

At once the ogre changed into a little mouse, and the cat pounced on him and ate him up!

Then the cat went into the castle. He told all the servants that their new master was the Marquis of Carabas, and that the king was coming to visit them.

When the king arrived at the castle, the cat purred, "Your Majesty, welcome to the home of the Marquis of Carabas."

The cunning cat told his master to ask the king for his daughter's hand in marriage. And that's what he did!

The king, impressed by the nobleman's wealth, agreed and soon the Marquis of Carabas and the princess were married.

The cat was made a lord of their court and was given the most splendid clothes, which he wore proudly with his fine boots. And they all lived happily ever after.

The Story of the Blue Jackal

Once upon a time, there lived a jackal named Chandarava. One day, he was very hungry. He couldn't find any food in the jungle, so he wandered into a nearby village to search for something to eat.

The dogs in the village saw him and started to chase him. Trying to escape, Chandarava ran into a house. It belonged to a washerwoman. Inside was a big vat of blue dye. Without thinking, Chandarava jumped into the vat to hide. His entire body was dyed blue. When he climbed out, he no longer looked like a jackal.

The dogs were confused. They had never seen a blue animal before. Terrified, they ran away.

Hungry and fed up, Chandarava returned to the jungle. The blue dye wouldn't wash off! When the other animals saw him, they were frightened and ran away. Chandarava didn't want to be alone, so he came up with a clever plan.

"Don't be afraid," said the blue creature. "The Lord of Creations has sent me here to be your king and to protect you.

Come and live in peace in my kingdom."

The other animals were convinced by Chandarava's words.

"O, Master, we await your commands. Please let us know whatever you want," they said.

The blue jackal gave everyone jobs – mostly to serve him! He enjoyed being treated like royalty, but he was also a kind and fair ruler, and the animals lived peacefully together.

One evening, after enjoying a particularly fine feast, Chandarava heard a pack of jackals howling in the distance.

Unable to hide his natural instinct, Chandarava howled back. When the other animals heard this, they realised that Chandarava was only a jackal and not the king he was pretending to be.

Chandarava knew he had been wrong to fool the animals. He tried to explain why he had lied, but it was too late. The animals were so angry that they chased him out of the jungle.

So the blue jackal ended up spending the rest of his days alone after all.

The Princess and the Pea

Once upon a time, a king and queen lived in their castle with their only son. They were growing old, and it wouldn't be long before the prince would need to take up the throne. But before he became king, the prince wanted to find a princess to be his wife. He wanted her to be clever and funny and loving and kind.

The prince travelled the world in search of a real princess, but none of the princesses he met was quite right.

Then, one stormy night, there was a loud knock on the castle door.

"Who could be out on such a terrible night?" cried the queen.

The king rose to his feet. "Whoever it is, we must let them in and offer them shelter."

The prince helped his father pull open the castle's heavy doors. To their astonishment, a girl was standing outside, shivering in the rain.

"Good evening," she said politely. "Please may I come in? I was travelling when I lost my way. I'm cold and wet."

"You poor thing," cried the queen. "You must stay here."

The prince could not stop staring at the beautiful girl. "What's your name?" he asked.

"I'm Princess Sophia," she replied.

At the word 'princess', the king looked at the queen. The queen smiled and took the girl's hand.

"Let's get you some dry clothes," she said.

That evening, over supper, the prince chatted with the charming girl. She was everything he had dreamed of, and by the end of the evening he had fallen in love!

The queen was happy for her son, but she wanted to make sure Sophia was a real princess.

She got her maid to help her pile up twenty mattresses on the guest bed. Under the bottom mattress she placed a tiny pea.

Then the queen showed Sophia to her room. "Sleep well, my dear," she said.

The next morning, the queen asked Sophia how she had slept. Sophia looked pale and tired.

"Not too well, I'm afraid," said the girl. "There was a hard lump in the bed and now I'm covered in bruises."

On hearing these words, the queen laughed and hugged Sophia tightly.

"We have found our princess!" she cried. "Only a real princess would be delicate enough to feel a tiny pea through so many mattresses!"

"I knew it!" grinned the king.

The prince dropped down on one knee.

"Sophia, would you do me the honour of marrying me?" he asked.

Princess Sophia's eyes sparkled with happiness.

"Yes," she nodded. "I will!"

The prince married his bride that very day and they all lived happily ever after.

This all happened a long time ago. If you are passing by the castle, be sure to visit its museum. There's a very special exhibit on display, in a dusty glass case – a tiny, shrivelled pea! Proof of a real princess.

Pinkabella and the Fairy Goldmother

Pinkabella loved pink almost more than anything else…
and she loved LOTS of things, like playing with her friend,
Violet, and spending time with her godmother, Auntie Alura.

Pinkabella often thought her auntie might be a fairy
godmother. She always looked so sparkly and magical!

One day, while Pinkabella and Violet were playing in
Pinkabella's bedroom, Auntie Alura came to visit.

"Auntie," cried Pinkabella, flying into her godmother's arms.

"It's lovely to see you too, Pinkabella," Auntie Alura laughed,
hugging her back. "Is this your room? It's very…"

"PINKTASTIC!" beamed Pinkabella.

"PINKERRIFiC!" added Violet.

"Er, yes," said Auntie Alura, casting her eye around Pinkabella's things. "Although I've always preferred gold, myself!"

Pinkabella looked at her auntie's gold dress, gold shoes and gold bag, and grinned. Auntie Alura really did like gold!

"Maybe she's my fairy GOLDmother," Pinkabella whispered to Violet with a giggle.

Just then, Pinkabella's dad called up from the garden. "Pinkabella! Violet! Come and get a drink." And the two friends rushed downstairs, leaving Auntie Alura alone in the bedroom.

A while later, after Auntie Alura had joined them outside, Pinkabella and Violet returned upstairs.

"Eek!" gasped Pinkabella as she opened her bedroom door. "My pinktacular room is all...GOLD!"

"B-but how?" asked Violet, in shock.

Suddenly, Pinkabella saw a sparkly stick on her bed.
"This looks like a wand," she gasped.
"Do you think it's magic?" asked Violet.
Pinkabella grabbed the stick. "Let's try it!"
She waved the wand and said, "Make everything
PINKTASTIC again!"
The wand made a fizzing noise, and pink sparkles
shot out of the end…

The sparkles whizzed through the air, and everything they landed on turned bright pink.

"Wow! It IS real," cried Violet. "Let me have a go!"

Pinkabella threw the wand to Violet, but it bounced off the wall and flew out of the open window.

Pinkabella and Violet watched in horror as the wand twirled away, shooting pink sparkles down into the garden.

Pinkabella and Violet ran outside. Everything had turned pink, including Pinkabella's mum, dad and auntie!

"My wand!" cried Auntie Alura. "What's it doing out here?"

"I found it on my bed," replied Pinkabella. "I'm really sorry, Auntie Alura. I didn't know it was your wand. I just wanted my room to be pink again."

"It's okay. I'm sorry, too," said her auntie. "I wanted to see what your room would look like in gold, but then I forgot to change it to pink again. I must have left my wand behind by mistake."

After Auntie Alura had turned everything back to normal, Pinkabella asked her why she had a wand.

"I'm your fairy godmother, of course," she whispered. Pinkabella gasped in delight. She had been right all along!

Then Auntie Alura added a touch of gold to Pinkabella's dress.

"Pink and gold together," laughed Pinkabella. "It's magical!"

Ella's Year

Ella's daddy always moaned about the weather.

"It's too windy," he grumbled in spring. Ella laughed. "Wind is fun," she said, helping him to fly a kite high in the air.

In summer, Daddy didn't want to play outside.

"It's too hot," he said. "I need to cool down."

"Sunny days are fun," said Ella. She held Daddy's hand and they ran to the cool, blue sea for a splash and a paddle.

When autumn came, Daddy frowned.

"The fallen leaves are too messy," he complained.

"They're beautiful," said Ella. She showed him how to rustle and crunch through the leaves on the walk to school.

Soon, winter arrived.

"It's too cold," said Daddy. "There's nothing good about winter."

"Winter is the best season of all," said Ella, and she pulled him outside to build a snowman.

Daddy laughed. "I may not always like the weather," he said, "but I love playing with you, Ella!"

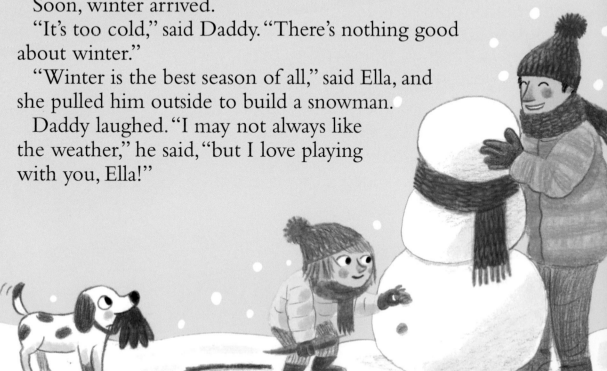

Rosie's Surprise

Rosie longed to ride a horse at the stables, just like her brother, Ben. But Ben only let his sister muck out the stalls.

"You don't know anything about horses," he told her. "You can watch me ride while you clean."

Then, one morning, when Ben was trying to ride his newest horse, it refused to budge or do anything it was told.

"I bet I can help," thought Rosie.

So the next day, she got up early and went to see Ben's newest horse. Instead of jumping on its back straightaway, like Ben did, Rosie spent time grooming its coat and talking in a soothing voice. Soon, she and the horse were friends. When Ben arrived, Rosie was trotting around the stable yard on its back.

"Rosie," cried Ben, "you're amazing!"

"So, can I can ride your horse too?" Rosie asked.

Ben laughed. "Yes, and I'll muck out the stalls today. I want to watch you and learn some tips!"

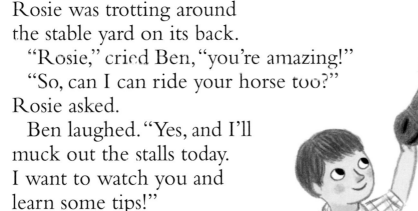

Cinderella

Once upon a time, there was a young girl who lived with her father, stepmother and two stepsisters. The stepmother was unkind, and the stepsisters were mean. They made the girl do all the housework, eat scraps and sleep by the fireplace among the cinders and ashes. Because she was always covered in cinders, they called her 'Cinderella'.

One morning, a special invitation arrived. All the young women in the kingdom were invited to a royal ball – a ball for the prince to choose a bride!

Cinderella longed to go, but her stepsisters just laughed.

"You? Go to a ball? In those rags? How ridiculous!" they cackled.

Instead, Cinderella had to rush around helping her stepsisters get ready for the ball.

As they left for the palace, Cinderella sat beside the fireplace and wept.

"I wish I could go to the ball," she cried.

Suddenly, a sparkle of light filled the dull kitchen, and a fairy appeared!

"Don't be afraid, my dear," she said. "I am your fairy godmother, and you SHALL go to the ball!"

"But how?" said Cinderella.

"Find me a big pumpkin, four white mice and a rat," replied the fairy godmother.

Cinderella found everything as quickly as she could. The fairy godmother waved her wand and the pumpkin changed into a magnificent golden coach, the white mice became white horses and the rat became a coachman.

With one last gentle tap of her wand, the fairy godmother changed Cinderella's dusty dress into a shimmering ball gown. On her feet were two sparkling glass slippers.

"Now, off you go," said the fairy godmother, "but remember, all this will vanish at midnight, so make sure you are home by then."

Cinderella climbed into the coach, and it whisked her away to the palace.

Everyone was enchanted by the lovely stranger, especially the prince, who danced with her all evening. As Cinderella whirled round the room in his arms, she felt so happy that she completely forgot her fairy godmother's warning.

Suddenly, she heard the clock strike midnight...
BONG... BONG... BONG...

Cinderella picked up her skirt and fled from the ballroom.
The worried prince ran after her.

BONG... BONG... BONG... She ran down the palace steps,
losing a glass slipper on the way, but she didn't dare stop.

BONG... BONG... BONG... Cinderella jumped into the
coach, and it drove off before he could stop her.

BONG... BONG... BONG!

On the final stroke of midnight, Cinderella found herself
sitting on the road beside a pumpkin, four white mice and a
black rat. She was dressed in rags and had only a single glass
slipper left from her magical evening.

At the palace, the prince saw something twinkling on the steps — a single glass slipper!

"I will marry the woman whose foot fits this glass slipper," he declared.

The next day, the prince took the glass slipper and visited every house in the kingdom.

At last, the prince came to Cinderella's house. Her stepsisters tried and tried to squeeze their huge feet into the delicate slipper, but no matter what they did, they could not get the slipper to fit. Cinderella watched as she scrubbed the floor.

"May I try, please?" she asked.

"You didn't even go to the ball!" laughed the elder stepsister.

"Everyone may try," said the prince, as he held out the sparkling slipper. And suddenly...

"Oh!" gasped the stepsisters, as Cinderella's dainty foot slipped easily into it.

The prince joyfully took Cinderella in his arms.

"Will you marry me?" he asked.

"I will!" Cinderella said.

Much to the disgust of her stepmother and stepsisters, soon Cinderella and the prince were married.

They lived long, happy lives together, and Cinderella's stepmother and stepsisters had to do their own cleaning and never went to a royal ball again.

Why the Sun and the Moon Live in the Sky

Long ago, the Sun and the Water were great friends, and they both lived on the Earth together. The Sun visited the Water often, but the Water never returned his visits.

At last the Sun asked his friend why he never visited. The Water replied that the Sun's house was not big enough, and that if he came with all his family, he would drive the Sun out of his home.

"If you want me to visit you," the Water added, "you will have to build a very large house. I have a huge family and we take up a lot of room."

The Sun promised to build a very large house and soon afterwards, he returned home to his wife, the Moon.

The Sun told the Moon what he had promised the Water, and the next day, they began building a large house to entertain the Water and all his family.

After several weeks, the house was complete and the Sun asked the Water to come and visit him.

When the Water arrived, he called out to the Sun and asked whether it would be safe to enter.

"Yes, of course. Come in," replied the Sun.

The Water began to flow in, followed by the fish and all the other animals and creatures that belonged to the Water.

Very soon, the Water was knee-deep in the house.

"Is it still safe for us to come in?" called out the Water.

"Yes, of course," replied the Sun. So more of the Water's family came in.

When the Water was at the level of a man's head, the Water said to the Sun, "Do you want more of my family to come?"

Not knowing any better, the Sun and the Moon both said that everyone was welcome. More and more of the Water's family came in, until the Sun and the Moon had to sit on top of their roof.

Every so often, the Water asked the Sun if it was still okay to come in. Each time, the Sun and the Moon answered yes.

Soon, the Water overflowed the top of the roof, and the Sun and the Moon couldn't see their house any more.

As the Water rose higher and higher, the Sun and the Moon climbed up into the sky…and they've been there ever since!

165

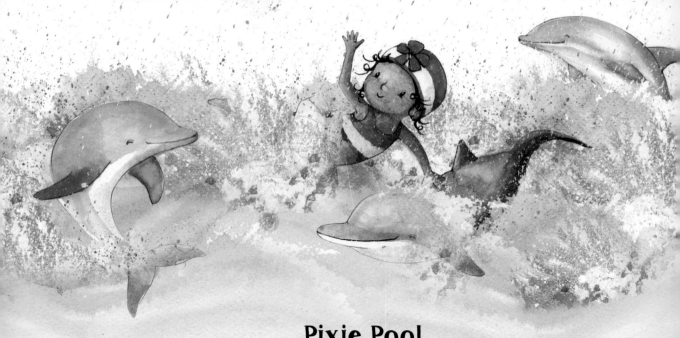

Pixie Pool

Lilian wasn't enjoying her day at the beach.
"I'll never learn to swim," she said. Even with floats and armbands, Lilian found swimming tricky. So she went to explore some rock pools. One of them sparkled like diamonds. When Lilian peered more closely, she saw a pixie sitting beside the pool. Lilian gasped in surprise.

"Please don't tell anyone you saw me!" cried the pixie. "If you keep my secret, I'll grant you a wish. What will it be?"

"Please can you make me swim as gracefully as a dolphin?" Lilian asked.

The pixie smiled. Just then, Lilian heard dolphin voices calling to her from the sea. "We'll help you!" they said.

Lilian splashed into the water and the dolphins jumped and dived around her.

"This is fun!" Lilian said, joining in. Suddenly, she was gliding through the water, just like the dolphins.

When they left, Lilian waved and carried on splashing. She couldn't wait for her next beach trip!

Show Time!

Isabelle the rabbit and her friends looked forward to the woodland summer show all year long. But this year, there was a problem.

"The show's cancelled!" cried Hazel the mouse. "This year's act, The Amazing Moles, are all ill in bed."

The other animals felt gloomy – except Isabelle.

"We're not giving up that easily," she said. "We can put on the show."

"How?" asked Magnus the squirrel.

"Practice makes perfect," said Isabelle.

So the friends rehearsed their favourite dance routines, jokes and magic tricks, while the audience gathered. Then the show began with a tap dance by Hazel and her sister Jessica. Magnus told jokes, and Gabriel the owl did magic. Finally, Isabelle performed a ballet dance. The crowd went wild!

"Being in the show was even more fun than watching it," said Isabelle, hugging her friends. "Let's do it again next year!"

Follow the Trail

Once upon a time there was a pair of tiger cub twins called Tia and Timus. They lived on the edge of the jungle with their mother. One day, Tia asked their mother if they could go down to the waterhole on their own.

"Yes," agreed Mother Tiger. "But don't stray from the path."

So Tia and Timus headed straight for the waterhole and played happily in the shallows.

As they were splashing around, they heard something hissing in the undergrowth.

"Hey, it's a snake," cried Timus. "Let's go snake hunting."

"Yes," cried Tia, leaping out of the water. And, forgetting all about their mother's warning, the two tiger cubs went charging deep into the jungle.

They raced on and on until they were quite out of breath.

"I don't think we'll ever find that snake, do you?" laughed Tia.

"No," agreed Timus. "And now I'm hungry and tired. Let's go home."

But when the tiger cubs looked around they discovered that they were quite lost.

"Oh, no," wailed Tia. "We'll never find the path again."

"We should have remembered Mummy's warning," cried Timus. The two cubs huddled together and trembled with fear.

They had heard all kinds of tales about the dangers that lurked in the jungle.

Suddenly, Timus noticed something on the ground.

"Look," he cried. "We've left a trail of wet footprints. All we need to do is follow them and we'll find our way back to the waterhole."

"Then we'll be able to find the path leading home," added Tia.

So the two tiger cubs very carefully followed the footprint trail back to the waterhole. Then they followed the path all the way home. They didn't even stop when they heard something scratching around in a hollow tree trunk.

They were so pleased when they saw their mother that they bounced on her and gave her a big hug.

"Hey, what was that for?" asked Mother Tiger.

"Because we love you," said Tia.

"And you are so terribly wise," added Timus.

From then on, Tia and Timus always did exactly what their mother told them.

The Snow Queen

Once, there was a wicked imp who made a magic mirror. Everything it reflected looked ugly and mean. One day, the mirror smashed into tiny specks, and the specks got into people's eyes and made everything look bad to them. Some specks became caught in people's hearts, making them feel grumpy.

A few of the specks from the mirror floated towards a far-away place where there lived two best friends, called Gerda and Kay.

The pair spent endless days together. In the winter, Gerda's grandmother told them wonderful stories while the snow swirled outside.

"The Snow Queen brings the winter weather," she would say. "She peeps in at the windows and leaves icy patterns on the glass."

In the summer, the children would play in the little roof garden between their houses.

One sunny day, they were reading together when Kay let out a cry. Specks from the imp's magic mirror had caught in Kay's eye and his heart.

Kay became bad-tempered throughout the summer and the autumn, and was still cross when winter came.

One snowy day, he stormed off with his sledge. Suddenly, a large white sleigh swept past and Kay mischievously hitched his sledge to the back.

The sleigh pulled him far, far away. When it finally stopped, Kay realised the sleigh belonged to the Snow Queen from Gerda's grandmother's story! The Snow Queen kissed Kay's forehead and her icy touch froze his heart. He forgot all about Gerda and his home.

Back home, Gerda missed Kay. She searched everywhere for him. Just as she was about to give up, Gerda noticed a little boat among the rushes down by the river.

"Perhaps the river will carry me to Kay," she thought. She climbed in and the boat glided away.

Many hours later, the boat reached the shore. A large raven came hopping towards Gerda.

"I have seen your friend," the raven croaked. "A young man who sounds like him has married a princess. I'll take you there."

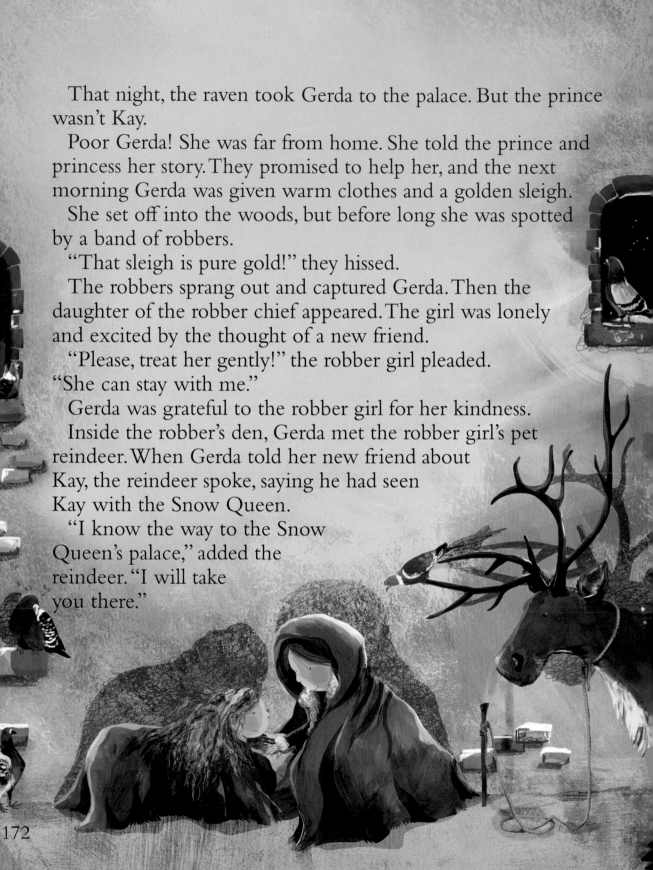

That night, the raven took Gerda to the palace. But the prince wasn't Kay.

Poor Gerda! She was far from home. She told the prince and princess her story. They promised to help her, and the next morning Gerda was given warm clothes and a golden sleigh.

She set off into the woods, but before long she was spotted by a band of robbers.

"That sleigh is pure gold!" they hissed.

The robbers sprang out and captured Gerda. Then the daughter of the robber chief appeared. The girl was lonely and excited by the thought of a new friend.

"Please, treat her gently!" the robber girl pleaded. "She can stay with me."

Gerda was grateful to the robber girl for her kindness.

Inside the robber's den, Gerda met the robber girl's pet reindeer. When Gerda told her new friend about Kay, the reindeer spoke, saying he had seen Kay with the Snow Queen.

"I know the way to the Snow Queen's palace," added the reindeer. "I will take you there."

It was a long, cold journey, but at last Gerda and the reindeer arrived outside the Snow Queen's palace.

Inside the ice palace, the Snow Queen still held Kay under her spell.

"Spring is coming," she announced suddenly. "I must leave. It is time for me to make it snow on the other side of the world!" And she flew off in her sleigh, leaving Kay alone.

At that moment, Gerda crept into the palace. When she saw her friend, she wept. Her tears fell onto his chest. They melted his cold heart and washed away the speck of glass. Kay began to cry too, and his tears washed the glass from his eye. At last he was free of the spell!

The reindeer carried Gerda and Kay back home.

"Grandmother!" called Gerda. "We're back at last!"

The old lady hugged them tightly. She was so happy to see them.

"I knew that you would come home one day," she cried. "Now, tell me all about your adventures!"

The Donkey and the Load of Salt

One day, a merchant went to collect some sacks of salt from the seashore. He piled the sacks onto the back of his donkey and they started to make their way home.

The donkey struggled to carry the heavy load, and as he crossed a shallow river he slipped on the wet stones. SPLOSH! The sacks tumbled into the water. By the time the man had picked them up, most of the salt had been washed away.

"That's better!" thought the donkey, as the man reloaded the half-empty sacks onto his back. And he trotted on happily down the road.

The following day, the merchant went back to the seashore to get more salt and loaded up the donkey once again.

Now, the donkey was very annoyed at having to carry another heavy load, so when they reached the river on their way home, he remembered what had happened the day before and pretended to slip. SPLASH! The sacks of salt fell into the water.

By the time the man had hauled them out, the sacks were half empty again, much to the donkey's delight.

The merchant, who was no fool, soon guessed that the donkey had slipped on purpose this time, and he was very angry. So he came up with a plan to teach the lazy creature a lesson.

The next day, he took the donkey to the seashore again, but this time he loaded two large baskets of sponges onto his back. Of course, the sponges were very light, but by the time they reached the river, the rough baskets were beginning to scratch the donkey's shoulders.

"I know, I'll pretend to slip again," thought the crafty creature – and WHOOPS! – he tipped the sponges into the river.

To the donkey's surprise, the merchant did not get angry. He just picked up the sponges and put them back in the baskets.

"Oh, no!" groaned the donkey, as the baskets filled up. The water-soaked sponges were so heavy! He had no choice but to struggle on home, carrying a load ten times heavier than before.

And the moral of the story is: one solution does not fit all problems.

The Fisherman and His Wife

One day, when the sea was blue and calm, a poor fisherman set off to work. At first, he caught nothing. Then, when the fisherman was about to call it a day, he felt a tug on his line. The fisherman struggled to reel it in.

"This must be a big fish," he thought.

The fish was enormous, and the fisherman was very pleased. But his pleasure turned to surprise when the fish spoke to him.

"Please throw me back," pleaded the fish. "I am not really a fish at all, but an enchanted prince."

The stunned fisherman gently let the fish back into the water and set off for home.

The fisherman and his wife were so poor that they lived in a wooden shed. When he told his wife about the talking fish, she was angry with him.

"You fool!" she cried. "No wonder we're so poor, if you can't see a good thing when it's biting you on the nose!"

The fisherman's wife told him that if the fish was an enchanted prince, he should have asked for something in return for setting him free.

"Go back to the same spot tomorrow and catch that fish again, and this time ask him for a little cottage so we can live a better life," said the fisherman's wife.

The next morning, when the sea was green and choppy, the fisherman set off again. He rowed out to the same spot as the day before, hoping to see the magical fish.

"Enchanted prince, please hear my plea, jump out from the water and talk to me," called the fisherman.

The fish appeared and asked the fisherman why he had called him. The fisherman explained that he was a very poor man and would like to live in a little cottage instead of a wooden shed.

"Go home," said the fish. "Your wish is granted." And he left with a SPLISH!

So the fisherman returned to his wife, who waved to him from the window of their lovely new cottage.

The fisherman's wife was pleased for a little while, but soon became unhappy again.

"We could have asked for more from that magic fish," she told her husband one evening. "This is only a small cottage; a castle would be much better." And she begged her husband to go and find the magical fish, and ask him to grant her wish.

177

The next morning, when the sea was purple and rough, the fisherman set off again and rowed out to the same spot as before.

"Enchanted prince, please hear my plea, jump out from the water and talk to me," called the fisherman.

The fish appeared, although he didn't seem very happy about being called again. The fisherman explained that his wife found the cottage rather small, and would prefer to live in a castle.

"Go home," said the fish. "Your wish is granted." And he left with a SPLASH!

So the fisherman returned to his wife, who waved to him from the window of a grand castle.

But the fisherman's wife wanted even more. "If that fish can give us a grand castle, he can make me a queen," she said.

The next morning, when the sea was grey and murky, the fisherman set off again and rowed out to the same spot as before.

"Enchanted prince, please hear my plea, jump out from the water and talk to me," called the fisherman.

The fish appeared, not at all pleased to be called again. The fisherman explained that his wife now wanted to be a queen.

"Go home," said the fish. "Your wish is granted." And he left with a SPLOSH!

So the fisherman returned to his wife, now a queen.

"If that fish can make me a queen, then he can make me the ruler of the whole world!" said the fisherman's wife.

The next morning, when the sea was black and stormy, the fisherman rowed out to the same spot as before.

"Enchanted prince, please hear my plea, jump out from the water and talk to me," called the fisherman.

The fish appeared. He was furious. The fisherman explained that his wife now wanted to be the ruler of the world.

"Go home," said the fish. "Your wife has what she deserves." And he left with a SPLISH, SPLASH, SPLOSH!

The fisherman returned to his wife... who was living in the wooden shed again.

Her greed had indeed been rewarded!

How Butterflies Came to Be

One day, a long time ago, Elder Brother, the spirit of goodness, was out walking. The summer was over, the sky was blue, and everywhere he looked he saw the colours of autumn.

Soon Elder Brother arrived at a village where the women were grinding corn and children were playing happily together. He sat down feeling very content, as he enjoyed the beautiful autumn colours and the sound of birdsong.

Suddenly, Elder Brother became sad. "It will be winter soon," he thought. "The colourful autumn leaves will shrivel and fall, and the flowers will fade."

Elder Brother tried to think of a way to keep the autumn colours, so that everyone could enjoy them for longer.

Wherever he went, Elder Brother always carried a bag. Now he opened it up and started to fill it with the colours he saw all around him.

He took gold from a ray of sunlight and blue from the sky. He collected shiny black from a woman's hair and white from the cornmeal. He took green from the pine needles, red and yellow from the leaves, and purple and orange from the flowers.

When all the colours were in the bag, Elder Brother shook it. Then he thought of something else. He heard the birds singing and added their songs to the bag.

Elder Brother called the children over.

"I have a surprise for you!" he told them. "Take this bag and open it."

The children opened the bag, and hundreds of colourful butterflies flew out. How the children laughed with joy!

The women came over to see the butterflies too, and so did the men who had been working in the fields. Everyone stretched out their hands so the butterflies could land on them, and the butterflies started to sing as they fluttered around.

The people were delighted, but the birds were angry. One bird perched on Elder Brother's shoulder.

"Why have you given our songs to the butterflies?" the bird asked. "We were each given our own song and now you've given them away to creatures that have more beautiful colours than we do."

Elder Brother agreed and apologised to the birds. He took the songs away from the butterflies and gave them back to the birds.

And that is how butterflies came to be – and why they are silent.

Alice and the White Rabbit

One day, Alice was sitting beside a river with her sister when something curious happened – a white rabbit with pink eyes ran past.

"Oh dear! Oh dear! I shall be too late!" he said. Then he took a watch out of his vest pocket and hurried on.

Alice followed the rabbit down a large rabbit hole. The rabbit hole went straight on like a tunnel for some way and then dipped so suddenly that she found herself falling down…

"I must be getting near the centre of the Earth," Alice thought to herself. Down, down, down Alice kept falling.

Suddenly, she landed in a heap at the bottom. When she got up, she found herself in a long hall, lined with doors. At the end was a little three-legged glass table. There was nothing on it but a tiny golden key. Alice tried the key in all the doors, but it wouldn't open any of them. Then she noticed a low curtain she had not seen before. Behind it was a tiny door.

She turned the key in the lock and it opened. The door led into a beautiful garden, but Alice could not even get her head through the doorway.

She went back to the table and saw a little bottle labelled "DRINK ME!"

Alice drank it and shrank. But she remembered that she had left the key on the table. Alice didn't know what to do. Then, she saw a cake marked "EAT ME!"

Alice ate it and began to grow. Soon, she was so large that her head touched the ceiling!

Alice began to cry. She was wondering what to do when who should come along but the white rabbit? He was carrying a pair of white gloves and a large fan.

"If you please, sir…" began Alice.

The rabbit dropped the gloves and fan, and scurried away.

"How strange everything is today," said Alice, picking up the gloves and the fan. "I'm not myself at all." Then she began fanning herself as she wondered who she might be instead.

After a while, Alice looked down at her hands. She was surprised to see that she had put on one of the rabbit's little white gloves.

"I must be growing smaller again," she thought.

Alice realised that it was the fan that was making her shrink, so she dropped it quickly and ran to the door. Suddenly, she remembered that the key was still on the table.

"Drat," she said. "Things can't possibly get any worse." But she was wrong. SPLASH! She fell into a sea of her tears.

"I wish I hadn't cried so much!" wailed Alice.

Just then, she heard something splashing. It was a mouse.

"Do you know the way out of this pool?" asked Alice.

The mouse didn't reply.

"Perhaps he speaks French," thought Alice. So she began again. "Où est mon chat?" which was the first sentence in her French book and meant "Where is my cat?"

The mouse leaped out of the water in fright.

"I'm sorry!" cried Alice. "I didn't mean to scare you."

"Come ashore," said the mouse. "I'll tell you why cats frighten me."

By this time, the pool was crowded with birds and animals. There was a duck, a dodo, a parrot, an eaglet and other curious creatures too. Together, they all swam to the shore.

The birds and animals were dripping wet.

"Let's have a race," said the dodo. "It will help us to dry off." And he began to mark out a course.

Then everyone began, starting and stopping whenever they felt like it. It was impossible to tell when the race was over, but after half an hour they were all very dry.

"But who won the race?" asked the mouse.

"Everyone," said the dodo. "Alice will give out prizes." So Alice handed around some sweets she had in her pocket.

"But she must have a prize, too," said the mouse.

"What else do you have in your pocket?" asked the dodo.

Alice handed over a thimble and he gave it back to her, saying, "I beg you to accept this thimble."

Alice accepted as solemnly as she could and then they all sat down to hear the mouse's tale. But Alice was so tired, she just couldn't concentrate, and she drifted off to sleep.

The next moment, she woke to the sound of her sister's voice. "Wake up, Alice!" said her sister. "What a long sleep you've had!"

"I've had such a curious dream!" said Alice, who told her sister all about it. And what a wonderful dream it had been!

The Fox and the Crow

One day, a crow was flying past an open window when she spotted a tasty piece of cheese on the table. There was no one in the room, so she fluttered in and stole it! Then she flew up into the branches of a nearby tree, and was just about to eat the cheese when a fox appeared.

The fox was also particularly fond of cheese and he was determined to steal the crow's prize.

"Good morning, Mistress Crow," he greeted her. "May I say that you are looking especially beautiful today? Your feathers are so glossy and your eyes are as bright as sparkling jewels!"

The fox hoped that the crow would reply and drop the cheese, but she didn't even thank him for his compliments. So he tried again: "You have such a graceful neck and your claws are really magnificent. They look like the claws of an eagle."

Still the crow ignored him.

The fox could smell the delicious cheese and it was making his mouth water. He had to find a way to make the crow drop it.

At last he came up with a plan.

"All in all, you are a most beautiful bird," he said. "In fact, if your voice matched your beauty, I would call you the Queen of Birds. Why don't you sing a song for me?"

Now, the crow liked the idea of being addressed as the Queen of Birds by all the other creatures in the woods. She thought that the fox would be very impressed by her loud voice, so she lifted her head and started to caw.

Of course, as soon as she opened her beak, the piece of cheese fell down, down, down to the ground. The fox grabbed it in a flash and gobbled it up.

"Thank you," he said. "That was all I wanted. I have to say that you may have a loud voice, but you don't have a very good brain!"

And the moral of the story is: be wary of a flatterer.

Balloon Carnival

Freddie had always wondered what it would be like to fly like a bird. One evening, he talked to his dad about it.

"Oh, it would be amazing!" said Dad. "Looking down on the world, soaring through the clouds...I know, why don't we organise a balloon ride, then we can see for ourselves!"

"That would be awesome, Dad!" cried Freddie, excitedly. "We'll be able to see everything from a bird's-eye view."

So a few days later, on a warm, breezy evening, Freddie and his dad set off on their balloon adventure.

They settled into the big wicker basket, and then they were off...floating higher and higher. Up, up and away in the big pink balloon!

Freddie couldn't believe his eyes...

Up above, he could see planes soaring through the clouds.

"I wonder where they are going?" he sighed, as he watched their fluffy vapour trails fade into the distant sun-tinted skies.

"Look over there, Freddie," cried Dad, pointing at a flock of birds.

They soared past, flying in a V formation.

As the breeze rustled through his hair, Freddie glanced down. Everything looked tiny! Houses and trees appeared in miniature, like models. The cars crawled along winding ribbons of roads like marching ants.

Dad grinned at Freddie. "How are you enjoying your ride?" he asked.

"It's so cool," laughed Freddie. "I feel like I'm a bird, too. I can't believe we are so high in the air!"

The balloon drifted along silently and over the crest of a hill. Suddenly, the sky was filled with other balloons of all shapes and sizes. Freddie could see a smiling elephant and an inflated bear with a sleepy face. Hovering nearby was a shimmering butterfly and a funny bunny balloon.

"A balloon carnival!" cried Dad, smiling and waving as they floated along on the breeze with the other balloons.

Freddie glanced off into the distance. He could see the silhouette of a city, and the sun was beginning to dip towards the horizon. It was time to head home.

Slowly, the balloon glided lower and lower, down and down… until it landed with a gentle bump on the ground.

Freddie hugged his dad.

"Thanks, Dad," he said. "This has been the best day EVER!"

Dad smiled. "Let's go on another balloon adventure soon."

The Vain Swan

Once upon a time four beautiful swans lived on a big river. The swans were the best of friends and were very happy. They looked so graceful and lovely that people always stopped to admire them. Then one day, something happened. Felix, the youngest swan, noticed his reflection for the first time. He was very pleased with what he saw and began to boast about how handsome he was.

"Look at my fine feathers," he said vainly. "I have the whitest feathers of any swan on the river. I'm sure all the people come here to look at me. They're not interested in ordinary swans, like the rest of you."

At first the older swans tried to ignore him. But Felix kept staring at his reflection and remarking upon his beauty. Before too long, the other swans got fed up and decided to teach him a lesson.

"If people only come to see YOU," they honked, "then we don't need to stay here. We can find somewhere else fit for ordinary swans." And off they flew.

At first, Felix was so busy admiring his reflection that he didn't really miss his friends. But, of course, it wasn't long before he started to feel very lonely. He hung his head and paddled sadly along the river.

The people who came down to the river couldn't help noticing that something was wrong. "Where have the other fine swans gone?" they asked. "There's only one sad-looking swan left."

After many days, Felix realised how silly he had been. He knew he had to do something, so he soared into the sky.

Over the countryside he flew, in search of his friends. At last he saw three beautiful swans swimming on a fine lake. He swooped down shyly, afraid that they would send him away.

"I've missed you," he told them. "I'm sorry I was so vain and silly."

Of course, his friends didn't chase him away. They were delighted to see him. "We've missed you, too," they honked. "Why don't you stay with us ordinary swans?"

Felix was overjoyed. "I'd love to," he honked in reply, "but... there is nothing ordinary about you!"

The Biggest Squeak in the World

Freddie couldn't squeak. Squeaking doesn't matter if you're a dog or a cat, but unfortunately Freddie was a mouse. And mice are supposed to squeak.

"All my friends can squeak," he said. "What's wrong with me?"

"You're just not ready yet," said his grandfather. "It will happen when the time is right."

Later that day, Freddie was moping outside the mouse hole when suddenly…HISS! A huge, hungry cat came springing towards him!

Freddie opened his mouth to yell for help – and instead let out an enormous SQUEAK! Every single mouse in the town heard it. Dogs heard it. Even humans heard it. The cat leaped into the air and all its fur stood on end. Then it shot away in terror.

When the other mice heard about the cat, they gave Freddie a big cheer.

"That's why your squeak took a long time to come," his grandfather laughed. "It's the biggest squeak in the world!"